PUCKING DISASTER

A WHY CHOOSE HOCKEY ROMANCE

CHARLOTTE BYRD

Copyright © 2023 by Byrd Books, LLC.

All rights reserved.

Proofreaders:

Renee Waring, Guardian Proofreading Services, https://www.facebook.com/GuardianProofreadingServices

No part of this book may be reproduced in any form or by any electronic or mechanical means, including information storage and retrieval systems, without written permission from the author, except for the use of brief quotations in a book review.

This book is a word of fiction. Names, characters, places, and incidents are either products of the author's imagination or are used fictitiously. Any resemblance to actual persons, living or dead, events, or locales is entirely coincidental. The author acknowledges the trademarked status and trademark owners of various products referenced in this work of fiction, which have been used without permission. The publication/use of these trademarks is not authorized, associated with, or sponsored by the trademark owners.

Visit my website at www.charlotte-byrd.com

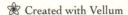 Created with Vellum

PRAISE FOR CHARLOTTE BYRD

"...tillation so masterfully woven, no reader can ...ist its pull. A MUST-BUY!" (*Goodreads*)

"...aptivating!" (*Goodreads*)

"...xy, secretive, pulsating chemistry…" (*Goodreads*)

"...arlotte Byrd is a brilliant writer. I've read loads ... I've laughed and cried. She writes a balanced ...k with brilliant characters. Well done!" (...odreads)

"...t, steamy, and a great storyline." (*Goodreads*)

"...oh my....Charlotte has made me a fan for life." (...dreads)

"...w. Just wow. Charlotte Byrd leaves me ...chless and humble… It definitely kept me on the ... of my seat. Once you pick it up, you won't put ...wn." (*Goodreads*)

"...rigue, lust, and great characters...what more ...d you ask for?!" (*Goodreads*)

"Twisted, gripping story full of heat, tension and action. Once again we are caught up in this phenomenal, dark passionate love story that is full of mystery, secrets, suspense and intrigue that continues to keep you on edge!" (Goodreads)

"Must read!" (Goodreads)

"Charlotte will keep you in suspense!" (Goodreads)

"Twisted love story full of power and control!" (Goodreads)

"Just WOW...no one can weave a story quite like Charlotte. This series has me enthralled, with such great story lines and characters." (Goodreads)

"Charlotte Byrd is one of the best authors I have had the pleasure of reading, she spins her storylines around believable characters, and keeps you on the edge of your seat. Five star rating does not do this book/series justice." (Goodreads)

"Suspenseful romance!" (Goodreads) ⭐⭐⭐⭐⭐

"Amazing. Scintillating. Drama times 10. Love and heartbreak. They say what you don't know can't hurt you, but that's not true in this book." (Goodreads) ⭐⭐⭐⭐⭐

"I loved this book, it is fast paced on the crime plot, and super-hot on the drama, I would say the perfect mix. This suspense will have your heart racing and your blood pumping. I am happy to recommend this thrilling and exciting book, that I just could not stop reading once I started. This story will keep you glued to the pages and you will find yourself cheering this couple on to finding their happiness. This book is filled with energy, intensity and heat. I loved this book so much. It was super easy to get swept up into and once there, I was very happy to stay." (*Goodreads*) ⭐⭐⭐⭐⭐

"BEST AUTHOR YET! Charlotte has done it again! There is a reason she is an amazing author and she continues to prove it! I was definitely not disappointed in this series!!" (*Goodreads*) ⭐⭐⭐⭐⭐

"LOVE!!! I loved this book and the whole series!!! I just wish it didn't have to end. I am definitely a fan for life!!! (*Goodreads*) ⭐⭐⭐⭐⭐

"Extremely captivating, sexy, steamy, in intense!" (*Goodreads*) ⭐⭐⭐⭐⭐

"Addictive and impossible to put down. ⭐⭐⭐⭐⭐

"What a magnificent story from the 1st through book 6 it never slowed down a surprising the reader in one way or the Nicholas and Olive's paths crossed in a unorthodox way and that's how their s it's exhilarating with that nail biting su keeps you riding on the edge the whole love it!" (*Goodreads*) ⭐⭐⭐⭐⭐

"What is Love Worth. This is a great e this series. Nicholas and Olive have a connection and the mystery surroundi of the people he is accused of murderi read. Olive is one strong woman with convictions. The twists, angst, confusi together to make this worthwhile read ⭐⭐⭐⭐⭐

"Fast-paced romantic suspense filled turns, danger, betrayal, and so much (*Goodreads*) ⭐⭐⭐⭐⭐

"Decadent, delicious, & dangerously (*Goodreads*) ⭐⭐⭐⭐⭐

WANT TO BE THE FIRST TO KNOW ABOUT MY UPCOMING SALES, NEW RELEASES AND EXCLUSIVE GIVEAWAYS?

Sign up for my newsletter and get a FREE book: https://dl.bookfunnel.com/gp3o8yvmxd

Join my Facebook Group: https://www.facebook.com/groups/276340079439433/

Bonus Points: Follow me on BookBub and Goodreads!

ABOUT CHARLOTTE BYRD

Charlotte Byrd is the bestselling author of romantic suspense novels. She has sold over 1.5 Million books and has been translated into five languages.

She lives near Palm Springs, California with her husband, son, a toy Australian Shepherd and a Ragdoll cat. Charlotte is addicted to books and Netflix and she loves hot weather and crystal blue water.

Write her here:

charlotte@charlotte-byrd.com

Check out her books here:

www.charlotte-byrd.com

Connect with her here:

www.tiktok.com/charlottebyrdbooks

www.facebook.com/charlottebyrdbooks

www.instagram.com/charlottebyrdbooks

Sign up for my newsletter: https://www.subscribepage.com/byrdVIPList

Join my Facebook Group: https://www.facebook.com/groups/276340079439433/

Bonus Points: Follow me on BookBub and Goodreads!

- amazon.com/Charlotte-Byrd/e/B013MN45Q6
- facebook.com/charlottebyrdbooks
- tiktok.com/charlottebyrdbooks
- bookbub.com/profile/charlotte-byrd
- instagram.com/charlottebyrdbooks
- x.com/byrdauthor

ALSO BY CHARLOTTE BYRD

All books are available at ALL major retailers! If you can't find it, please email me at charlotte@charlotte-byrd.com

Somerset Harbor
Hate Mate (Cargill Brothers 1)
Best Laid Plans (Cargill Brothers 2)
Picture Perfect (Cargill Brothers 3)
Always Never (Cargill Brothers 4)

Tell me Series
Tell Me to Stop
Tell Me to Go
Tell Me to Stay
Tell Me to Run
Tell Me to Fight
Tell Me to Lie

Tell Me to Stop Box Set Books 1-6

Black Series
Black Edge
Black Rules
Black Bounds
Black Contract
Black Limit

Black Edge Box Set Books 1-5

Dark Intentions Series
Dark Intentions
Dark Redemption
Dark Sins
Dark Temptations
Dark Inheritance

Dark Intentions Box Set Books 1-5

Tangled Series
Tangled up in Ice
Tangled up in Pain
Tangled up in Lace
Tangled up in Hate
Tangled up in Love

Tangled up in Ice Box Set Books 1-5

The Perfect Stranger Series

The Perfect Stranger
The Perfect Cover
The Perfect Lie
The Perfect Life
The Perfect Getaway

The Perfect Stranger Box Set Books 1-5

Wedlocked Trilogy
Dangerous Engagement
Lethal Wedding
Fatal Wedding

Dangerous Engagement Box Set Books 1-3

Lavish Trilogy
Lavish Lies
Lavish Betrayal
Lavish Obsession

Lavish Lies Box Set Books 1-3

All the Lies Series
All the Lies
All the Secrets
All the Doubts

All the Lies Box Set Books 1-3

Not into you Duet

Not into you
Still not into you

Standalone Novels
Dressing Mr. Dalton
Debt
Offer
Unknown

ABOUT PUCKING DISASTER

Three hot hockey players will do anything for her...
Can the four of them make it work?

I can't believe that I actually fell for three men at once. I never thought that this would ever happen.

Ash is the Southern Californian laid back surfer dude.

Soren is the exotic aloof Scandinavian.

Ryder is the tortured, brooding ex-foster kid from South Boston.

They're all possessive and obsessive but are willing to share me among themselves.

In order to make this work, we have to abide by a set of rules:

1. We're exclusive to each other.

2. We can't sleep with anyone else.

3. We can only be together when all four of us are together.

However, when Ash and Soren are sent up to the big leagues to play for the NHL's Seattle Orcas, our rules will be tested...

What happens when we're tempted? What happens when boundaries are blurred?

This is a why choose hockey romance with no cheating!

tropes:

- hockey romance
- why choose
- MFM
- new adult
- angsty/steamy
- workplace romance

1

HARLOW

"How have things been going for you? Have you given any thought to what we discussed in our last session?"

Max shrugs a little and averts his gaze like a guilty little boy. I already know what his answer is going to be before he opens his mouth. "I don't know how they could help."

I expected this. After all, I'm dealing with professional hockey players, men who would rather duke it out on the ice than talk about their feelings. "It can't hurt, right?"

"I know, but…" He rubs his hands over his jeans, frowning like they did something to insult him. "Talking into a mirror? No offense, but that's weird."

"They're called affirmations," I remind him as gently as I can. "They are very important. We discussed your self-image. How you feel about yourself, how you see yourself. And how the negative self-talk you absorbed when you were a kid informs your present-day beliefs. Practicing these affirmations in the mirror is the first step toward seeing yourself through new eyes."

"Yeah, but what if I don't believe the things you want me to say?"

I settle back in my chair, smiling gently. "You would not be the first person to ask that question. It means taking a leap of faith. Eventually, you say these things enough, and you start to believe them. They sink into your subconscious. Think of it this way, studies have shown that the majority of our brain activity takes place in the subconscious mind. It's going twenty-four-seven, nonstop. Our beliefs about ourselves, how we fit in the world… Whether we have what it takes to meet our full potential as a hockey player. Whether we have potential at all."

"You think my subconscious is what has me freezing up out there."

No pun intended, I'm sure. I doubt he would appreciate a joke, so I keep it to myself. "That's exactly what I think. Don't worry about how it might look to stare into your bathroom mirror every morning for just a few minutes at a time and remind yourself how valuable you really are. The team wouldn't have signed you if somebody didn't believe you have what it takes. But you're never going to level up until you get past these blocks you're struggling with."

He shoots me a sly look whose meaning I can guess pretty easily. "How many of the other guys are dealing with this?"

"You know I can't tell you that." A glance at the clock on my desk makes me sit up straighter. "And that's our time for this session. What do you think? Same time next week?"

"Yeah." He unfolds his very tall, broad body from the little chair and stretches.

"And don't forget your affirmations this time. Trust me just a little, okay? I wouldn't tell you to do anything that I didn't think was worth your time." It's obvious he's still not quite on board by the time I show him to the door, but he seems willing to try. After weeks of working with these stubborn guys, I know that's the best I can hope for.

I have only a short break scheduled between this session and a meeting with Coach Kozak to go over film from the most recent scrimmage games. When I took this job, I had no idea how many hours of film I might end up reviewing – though, sometimes, it's better to spend my time this way. Especially when there are certain team members going out of their way to avoid me. I can still do my job without feeling like I'm letting somebody down.

I can't exactly force any of the players to keep their appointments, but Ryder is skipping them outright. Maybe I should let Coach Kozak know he's canceled our last three scheduled sessions. If he were anybody else on the team, and the situation were any different, I would voice my concerns. Ryder is an exceptional player, and I would hate to see his self-sabotage translate into losing his contract with the team. Every day he spends ducking me is a day I worry he'll end up starting a fight at a bar, the way he's done before. No, I can't hover over him like a mother hen, but that won't stop me from worrying.

Especially when it's my fault he doesn't want to see me.

A glance at the sofa brings heat to my cheeks. No matter how long I live, I will never forget the blood-chilling moment when he walked in on me, completely naked, being serviced by two of his teammates. I could kick myself for being stupid enough to let that happen here in my office — for letting it happen at all, really. No matter how much fun it was, no matter how much I wanted it. We all did.

Was it worth the look of horror that washed over his face once he realized what he was looking at? No. I've had nightmares about it, being in that moment again, too shocked to defend myself – and with no way to defend myself, anyway. Not really. Once again, I went back on my word, and plunged headfirst into a huge mistake.

As far as I know, he hasn't raised any issues with Ash, or Soren, and something tells me I would know if he spread the word of what was going on here. Something tells me I would also be jobless, not to mention homeless since I'd have no way to continue paying my rent on that gorgeous three bedroom, two bath with a big yard and a sparkling pool.

Since I still have a job and a home, I guess I'm safe for now. If only I didn't wake up every morning wondering if this is the day the other shoe will drop and I'll be found out.

The coach is waiting for me in his office when I rap my knuckles against the open door. "That's one of the things I like best about you," he muses, motioning for me to enter. "You're so punctual."

"I don't want to keep you waiting. Lord knows you've got more than enough work to handle."

"Isn't that the truth?" Still, it seems like he's in a pretty good mood today, so I'll take that as a good sign as I settle in with the notebook I've been using to jot down thoughts about the players, and their weaknesses and strengths.

"How are the sessions going? I have to say, I've noticed some improvement during the scrimmages. Chris and Jake are working much better together."

"That's terrific. They seem to have an unspoken psychic connection, don't they? It's like they anticipate what the other needs without being told."

"And I never noticed it before," he confesses in his trademark gruff voice. "I guess we needed a fresh pair of eyes, eh?"

He's such a nice man, I can't stand hearing him get down on himself. "You've got a million and one things going on all the time and two dozen players to manage. You can't notice everything. I'm just glad I'm here to be that extra set of eyes."

I would never have expected to get along so well with a man like him. It didn't take long for me to figure out his gruff demeanor is only a thin shell covering a man I can best describe as a teddy bear.

We settle in to watch film from their latest scrimmage. "This bothers me." It only takes a minute or two for him to pause the film and tap the computer screen with the end of his pen. "Have you noticed this?"

What a lovely pit just formed in my stomach. Even with their helmets on, it's obvious who was involved in the slight skirmish during this particular game. It was nothing serious, just one of those little dust-ups that happens from time to time.

"Who is that?" I ask, stalling while my heart threatens to leap out of my chest. "I can't quite tell."

"It's Ryder and Ash." He goes back thirty seconds or so and replays the event. Did it suddenly get hot in here? Or is that guilt oozing its way out of me in the form of cold sweat?

"That was an aggressive move," I muse after watching Ryder slam Ash into the boards once again.

"Aggressive? He hit him like he wanted to hurt him. That's not like him. Against other teams, sure. But against his own teammate?" He shakes his head while a mournful expression settles over his weathered face.

I want to crawl into a hole and never come back. This is a nice man. A good, decent coach, who wants nothing but the best for his team. He has bent over backwards to make sure the guys treat me with respect and take seriously the work we're doing together. Sure, not all of them are fully committed yet, but they're at least trying. I know a lot of that has to do with the ground rules Coach Kozak set down from the beginning.

And here I am, pretending I don't have a clue why two of his best players almost got into a fight on the ice.

"I'll look into it," I offer as casually as I can. "I'm sure it's not anything serious. Ryder can shoot his mouth off sometimes, and so can Ash. It's probably something as simple as that."

"I hope you're right. I don't need their egos getting in the way of our plans for the team."

Our plans for the team. I love that he considers me a part of things.

And I hate to be the one undermining those plans. I know I can't take responsibility for Ryder's choices, but I will certainly take responsibility for hurting him. There I was, telling him we can't be together or even go out on a date, and he walked in on me with not one but two of his teammates.

It's obvious I'm going to need to get over my nerves and face him one-on-one, whether he wants to meet up or not. We both have a responsibility here.

I just hope he sees it that way.

2

HARLOW

This is just a barbecue. Something people do on hot days when they have a nice backyard and a pool. It doesn't have to be more than that.

Even I have to shake my head at my pitiful attempts at justifying this trip to Ash's house. When he invited me, promising it would be just the three of us – Soren included – I told myself it would be rude to turn him down and that this would be a good opportunity to find out how Ryder's been behaving in the locker room. Since neither of them came to me with any horror stories, I was naïve enough to believe he was doing all right. When will I learn just because I want things to be a certain way, it doesn't mean that's how they'll turn out?

In the backseat is a bag with a change of clothes and the enormous watermelon I picked up at the farmer's market with tonight in mind. The GPS takes me to an impressive, gated community– from the front gate I can barely make out a few impressive houses half-hidden by beautifully maintained trees and shrubs. Ash left my name at the front and the guard gives me a nod when he opens the gate.

It annoys me, the way my palms sweat and my nails tap the wheel. There's nothing to be nervous about. I'm glad for the chance to sit down with the guys and not worry about somebody overhearing us. I need to approach this as an opportunity to fix a problem at work. When I look at it that way, it only makes sense for me to show up.

Though the two-piece I'm wearing under my cover-up is another story. But hey, he's got a pool and said we would be swimming. What was I going to do, show up in a snowsuit? *That's right, Harlow. Keep telling yourself what you need to hear.* Yes, I'm sure there will be eye candy involved – they're not going to be wearing snowsuits, either. But we're adults. We can get through this without pawing at each other.

Famous last words.

Ash's house is as impressive as the others I passed on my way from the gate – a sprawling two stories with a lush lawn, and even colorful plants decorating the flowerbeds under the front windows. Beyond that is a fenced-off yard, which I now approach with my clothes over one shoulder, and the watermelon carried in both arms. I can't help but flash back to the movie *Dirty Dancing*, when Baby announces she carried a watermelon. Hopefully I won't be that awkward today.

The gate is open as Ash promised, but I announce myself loudly anyway. "Hello? I could use a little help with this thing." The aroma of grilled meat makes my mouth water as I round the rear of the house.

The first thing I see is Ash standing by the grill, a spatula in one hand. He whistles when he gets a look at the size of the melon. "Wow, the thing's a monster. I don't think the three of us could finish it."

"Speak for yourself." Soren is opening a bottle of white wine when he emerges from the house. I wonder if it came from his personal wine cellar. "I love watermelon. It'll be a miracle if the two of you get a piece."

This is nice. We're just coexisting like three friends. I can handle this. This does not have to devolve into an orgy or anything like that. No matter how tempted I am to ogle the guys in their swim trunks. I guess they figured wearing shirts would be a waste of time. *Down, girl. Remember how this usually turns out.* Right, with me, hating myself. I don't need that in my life. I don't want it, either.

I'm all too happy to let Soren take the watermelon off my hands — or arms, as it were. "I'll put it in the fridge, so it's nice and cold," he offers. "Help yourself to some wine." I do, reminding myself to take it slow on the booze. It's bad enough I have a weakness for these two. I don't need to get drunk and make things worse.

After pouring wine into a plastic cup, I treat myself to a look around the pleasant, comfortable yard with its lounge chairs and colorful umbrellas. "This is beautiful," I tell Ash as he flips burgers. "You spend a lot of time out here?"

"As much as I can manage. The pool is good therapy. Helps keep me stretched out and loose when I play." One thing I appreciate about him is how devoted he is to his performance on the ice. He knows he's lucky to be where he is, even if he wants to go further. He works hard and takes his job seriously. I can't say that for everyone else on the team, as much as I wish I could.

"Are you ready for some swimming after we eat?" he asks as he eyes me up and down. My skin erupts in goosebumps, but I play it cool.

"Sure. I've got my suit on under this." I tug at the loose, cotton cover-up.

"Damn. And there I was, hoping you'd be in the mood for a skinny dip." When all I do is quirk an eyebrow and scowl, he holds his hands up in surrender. "Sorry. I couldn't resist."

He's incorrigible, but I can't pretend not to like that about him. "What else is on the menu?"

"There's potato salad, deviled eggs, and corn on the cob."

"Sounds great. I'm starving."

"Patience." He offers a wink before the opening of the door draws our attention to Soren. *God give me strength.* The man could be chiseled from marble, if marble had a fantastic tan and moved with cat-like grace.

"Do you have peanut butter?" he asks Ash.

We exchange a quizzical glance. "Sure. Why?"

"I had a burger a couple weeks ago with peanut butter on it, and there was jelly on the side so you can dip it in."

"What?" I can't help laughing, shaking my head. "That sounds disgusting."

"It was out of this world. I'm telling you, you would love it."

"Peanut butter and jelly? I love it. Cheeseburgers? I love them, too. But together?" I scrunch up my face. "I can't imagine."

"Don't you dare desecrate one of my burgers with any of that," Ash warns, gesturing with the spatula. "I won't have my recipe ruined by an abomination like you just described."

I laugh again. "Wow, you're pretty serious about this, aren't you?"

"I have spent a lot of time crafting the perfect burger. We all have our thing." But he's laughing, too, so he can't be all that offended.

"Okay, Mr. Touchy. I just figured I'd help keep things interesting." I know I am not imagining the sly look Soren gives me after he says that. Something tells me I know what his definition of interesting is.

"Maybe I'll try a little bit on the side," I offer, then burst out laughing when Ash gasps like I just insulted him.

"You know what, I didn't know I was inviting two heathens to my home. Maybe I'm rethinking this whole barbecue idea."

It is so easy to laugh with them. So easy to relax. It's impossible not to when they're both so charming and funny and hot.

Maybe I need a dip in the pool right this very minute to cool off my overheated libido. Something tells me, though, that I could stay in there until I pruned from head to toe, and there would be no hope of cooling the endless attraction I feel for them both.

One thing I know for sure, I was wrong when I told myself I could bring Ryder into the conversation. All that will do is lead to the topic of the three of us in my office, and I don't want to do that. Maybe there's another way for me to figure out what's happening, and how I can bring a stop to it.

Besides, I'm already up to my neck in trouble with these two. I might need all my concentration to keep things from boiling over.

3

ASH

It would be a mistake to bring up the situation with Ryder.

When Soren gives me a pointed look as I'm taking the burgers from the grill, I shake my head. There's no question what's on his mind. When we talked about this, inviting her over and all that, it was only natural for Ryder to come up in the conversation. It's obvious he's got an issue with us right now—he damn near took my head off during our last scrimmage. But he hasn't said anything to either of us, not directly. It makes me wonder if he's waiting, or if he is too fucked up over the whole situation to do anything but pretend it didn't happen.

He sucks at pretending, if that's what he wants to do. Just because you don't mention something doesn't mean there aren't plenty of ways to bring it up.

The way I see it, if there were anything to talk about – a conversation between the two of them, that kind of thing — she would bring it up. If there's one thing I'm learning about the tempting Harlow, it's how rarely she keeps her thoughts to herself. I know she's freaked out over the whole thing, no matter how hard she tries to pretend like everything's okay. And when it comes down to it, I sort of feel like a selfish asshole for kissing her that day in her office. I acted on impulse and got things rolling. We could've gotten into a shit-ton of trouble.

Does any of that stop me from checking her out as we sit to enjoy our feast? Not even close. As much as I love nothing more than wrapping my lips around a thick, juicy burger, I'd much rather be eating her right now. The way she laughs, when she ducks her head and blushes when we flirt with her, the way she flirts back — I might have to make a quick trip to the bathroom to jerk off if there's any hope of making it through this without acting on impulse again.

"Okay." I wink at Harlow as I set the watermelon on the table once the burgers and everything else are nothing but a memory. "We'll see how much watermelon you can actually eat in one sitting."

Soren only shrugs as he picks up the big knife. "Don't say I didn't warn you. You might want to take everything you plan on eating now, before I get my hands on it."

I know what I would like to get my hands on. I have to bite my tongue to keep that one inside. Attraction aside, we're actually having fun chilling out, listening to music, talking baseball and the upcoming football preseason. I love the way her eyes light up and the enthusiasm that leaks into her voice when she talks about sports. It's obvious from her ease with the topic that she's well-versed. She's not one of those people who only pretends to know.

"Where do you find the time to follow so many teams?" I have to ask before biting into a slice of ruby red, juicy fruit. Soren was right to leave it in the fridge. There's not much that says summer like a cold watermelon on a hot day.

"You make time for the things you love. And I love sports."

"So football doesn't bore you? Or scare you?" Soren jokes, nudging her with his elbow.

She nudges him back. "What, do you think I'm a wuss? Like I can't take it? It's not like I'm out there taking the hits, you know."

"But seriously," I press, winking at Soren. "Does it get you off a little, watching the guys go head-to-head?"

"Oh, yeah." She rolls her eyes hard enough that I'm surprised they don't fall out of her head. "I totally get off on watching guys beat the crap out of each other. I'm more interested in a solid passing game and a wide receiver with good hands."

Here I go again, biting my tongue. I'll be lucky if it's still attached by the time she leaves. Soren's grimace tells me he's going through the same thing. At least he's trying to be on his best behavior, the way I am.

"I cannot eat another bite," she declares, wiping her hands on a napkin after polishing off three slices. "I am waving the white flag. This was all delicious."

"Yeah, you're not bad on the grill," Soren admits. "We should have a contest sometime. Grill versus grill. Who will reign supreme?"

"Oh, I would happily be a judge in a contest like that," Harlow offers. "Any excuse to sit down with some grilled food."

"Even if it has peanut butter and jelly on it?" I have to duck the napkin Soren throws at me.

"Sure, why not?," she decides with a shrug. "How do you know what you're missing out on if you don't try it?"

The way she first tried a threesome with us. I need to get over this. My brain can't function around this woman without every thought leading to sex. I'm starting to wonder if I have a serious problem.

Soren excuses himself and goes inside, and Harlow offers to help me clean up. "No, you're a guest," I insist. "Sit down and relax."

"Are you kidding? If I relax too much I'll end up falling asleep. I swear, I'm full enough to burst." She picks up our paper plates and napkins and tosses them in the trash bag I left outside for exactly that reason, humming to herself as she does. She has a light inside her – that's the only way I can describe it to myself. And everything somehow feels better, more special, when she's around. It's pretty pathetic, crushing like a hopeless school kid, but God knows I've tried to make myself forget the way she makes me feel. It's not possible. I sort of wish it was.

"What do you say about getting in the water?" I ask.

"I'm not sure I should. Aren't you supposed to wait after eating?"

"That's an old wives' tale."

"I don't know. The whole idea is you don't want to get a cramp while you're swimming."

"We're in a pool in my backyard, not the ocean," I remind her. "I think you'll be okay. Between the two of us, we'll keep you safe." For some reason, she frowns, and I hate to see it.

"Are you just afraid?" I tease, hoping to get a smile from her. "You said you weren't athletic, but you at least know how to doggy paddle, right?"

"Shut up!"

"I'm just saying. There's no shame in admitting your weaknesses. I think a therapist told me that once."

"Oh yeah?" she demands, hands on her hips. "Did she tell you what a jerk you are, too?"

"Who said the therapist was a she? Everybody knows men make the best therapists. Women are too emotional."

"You are such an ass!"

That's when she makes her mistake. When she lunges at me as I'm walking along the side of the pool. One second, she's pushing me with all her might, unaware that I was prepared for exactly that move.

The next minute, we're both tumbling into the pool once I grab a hold of her arm. She doesn't have time to scream before we hit the water.

She's screeching when we surface, splashing me when I reach out for her. "Dammit! You are the worst!"

"Says the girl who tried to push me into the water. What, you don't like getting a taste of your own medicine?"

"You're lucky I wasn't carrying my phone." She uses both hands to push wet hair away from her face, caught between sputtering and laughing. She only wants to pretend she's not having fun, to teach me a lesson or something like that. She has no idea how obvious it is.

She has no idea how irresistible she is. I mean, I couldn't keep my hands or my thoughts off her before this, when she was dry. What is it about a woman with slicked-back hair that turns me on so much?

She must read my thoughts as I close in on her. "Wait a second…"

"What?" I tease, coming closer.

"I know that look in your eye."

"What look?"

"The one where you look like you're ready to devour me."

"Now there's an idea I can get behind." And let her pretend all she wants, but I see the wicked gleam in her eye before I take her chin in my hand and press a soft kiss against her delectable lips. She lets out what could be a moan or a groan, depending on how

I want to interpret it – either way, it doesn't stop her from kissing me back with all the passion I know she has inside her.

"Hey. No fair. You got started without me." We break the kiss and look up to find Soren standing at the edge of the pool.

"Wait a second." She's all business again, putting space between us while she touches her hands to her flushed cheeks. "We didn't start anything. Nothing is starting."

"Sure," I grunt, taking her by the waist and pulling her close while Soren lowers himself into the pool. "Tell me another good one." It's one thing for her to have principles when we're not touching, but the second our mouths meet again she's putty in my hands, melting against me and opening her mouth when I probe with my tongue. When Soren approaches her from behind, she reaches behind her to grab hold of his head while we fight for control with our lips, our tongues.

I've started trouble all over again.

But I'm not going to pretend I'm sorry.

4

HARLOW

It's a lot easier once we're out of the pool and in Ash's room. As much fun as it is to get sexy in the water, it's also a little awkward.

We shouldn't be doing this at all — of course I know that, and I remind myself of it as I sit at the foot of the bed before reaching behind me to untie the straps holding up the top of my white bathing suit. I work my way back on my hands, watching the two of them as they lower their trunks, then climb onto the bed with me.

This shouldn't be happening. Then why does it feel so right? What is missing in me that I can't resist the opportunity to be touched and kissed by the two of them at once? I always thought I had everything together, that I wasn't missing anything. But here I am, sandwiched between two warm, muscular bodies, and I can't pretend there's anywhere else I'd rather be.

Soren nuzzles my neck before lapping along its length, and I moan in approval as heat unfurls in my core. Ash turns my face toward his to continue kissing me the way he'd done in the pool — slowly, deliberately. I could lie here like this all night, lost in sensory overload.

Then again, the almost painful ache between my thighs won't let me do that for long. I can't help but jerk my hips upward, yearning for more as my pussy grows wetter with every kiss, every stroke from Soren's tongue against my skin.

He grinds his hips, rubbing his erection against my hip. "What was that about not starting anything?" he asks as I take him in my hand and stroke him.

I don't want to think about that now. I don't want to think about anything. And by the time his precum helps me lube his length, he's not in the mood for conversation anyway.

Ash plays with my nipples, brushing his fingertips against them until I am almost whining, needy and desperate. Goosebumps erupt over my skin at the touch of his hot breath before he takes one of them between his lips and sucks.

"Let me have some of that," Soren murmurs, taking the other, and I could swear I've died and gone to heaven. It's almost too much, the sensations rolling through my body, the tension building in my core.

"That's right," I moan, running my hands through Ash's hair while I continue stroking Soren. "Suck them. You're both so good at that."

I can hardly believe my ears. Who am I? I've never been this demanding in bed – I have certainly never told a man to suck my nipples harder. And when they respond by doing exactly what I ask, the fresh heat that spreads through me has nothing to do with sex. It's powerful, this feeling. The sense that I can ask for what I want, and they'll give it to me, no questions asked. They're only too happy to pleasure me.

There have been so many times I've wanted to speak up and ask for what I want, but shame made it impossible. Good girls don't do things like that. Well, good girls don't do this, either. Maybe I'm not such a good girl, after all. Maybe I already knew that.

With a tug at the back of his head, I lift Ash's mouth from my nipple. "You can use that elsewhere, you know," I murmur, pressing on his shoulder to guide him further down my writhing body. "You're pretty good at sucking other things, if I remember correctly."

"If I'm dreaming, nobody wake me up." He throws my leg over his shoulder and parts my slick lips with his fingers before giving my clit the same treatment he did my nipple. I'm already close to the edge, grinding helplessly against his face while Soren begins fucking my fist.

That doesn't last long, though. "I need to be careful," he chuckles, getting up on his knees.

I hardly sound like myself as I turn my head toward his bobbing erection. "Bring it over here," I whisper, extending my tongue to catch a few glistening beads of moisture at his tip before taking him into my mouth.

"Holy shit," he grunts, holding the back of my head and pumping slowly in and out of my ready mouth. I catch a glimpse of his blissful expression an instant before Ash invades me with two digits, working them in and out of me while strumming my bundle of nerves with the tip of his tongue. It's too much, I can't take it, it's going to kill me. But I wouldn't stop it for anything, grinding against Ash in a frantic race to the finish.

I let Soren fall free once the familiar rush starts to break over me. "Yes!" I shout, shuddering as one blissful wave after another washes over my body. I'm floating in delicious darkness, where nothing matters but pleasure. Satisfaction.

Of course, they're not done with me, and I wouldn't expect them to be. Ash reaches over to pull condoms from the nightstand, one of which he tosses to Soren.

"What are you going to do to me now?" I whisper, my hunger growing again as I gaze lustfully at their chiseled bodies. They're like gods, both of them, and they both want me. The thought alone is enough to make me quiver in anticipation.

"What do you want us to do?" Soren mutters, and I respond by spreading my legs wider than ever.

"I want you to take turns on me," I tell him.

"I am loving this side of you." The two of them exchange a grin — one that quickly fades when I sit up.

"I want to be on top," I decide, because why not? Why not live out every fantasy while I have a chance? Soren is quick to lie down on his back and pull me on top of him, so I throw a leg over him and straddle his hips before guiding him inside me. Ash takes his place behind me, cupping my breasts, and massaging them as I slowly raise and lower myself.

"That's right," he mutters in my ear, his breath hot against my neck. "Take what you want. Whatever you want. It's yours." My body shudders at the idea while the heat already blazing in my pussy intensifies, making me grind hard against Soren's base.

"So hot," he whispers, running his hands over my thighs before using his thumb against my clit. Fireworks go off behind my eyelids, and suddenly I'm coming again, shouting out my release while Soren continues moving inside me, taking me from below.

But then Ash is quick to take his place and I move over to him, where he slides easily into me. Soren kneels beside me, holding my jaw in one big hand so he can plunder my mouth with his tongue. Ash can't stay still – he thrusts upward, hard, fast, pounding me until there's nothing I can do but scream into Soren's mouth. I don't know if I'm coming or not — it's like I'm at the edge of a cliff, everything heightened, and it goes on and on until tears roll down my cheeks. I don't know how much more I can take, I don't know if my body is capable of much more.

"Come on my cock," Ash grunts. Soren kisses and licks my neck while I look down at him to find him staring up at me, wearing a hard expression — teeth gritted, eyes narrowed to slits.

"Are you ready to do that?" Soren whispers in my ear before lapping at the lobe. In the middle of my confused arousal I realize he's toying with my ass, stroking it, teasing yet more sensation out of my already overloaded body. "Are you gonna come on his cock? Do you have another one for him?"

"Yes!" I sob, working for it, working both of us until there's nothing left to do but howl when another mind-blowing orgasm slams into me. Everything goes dark before exhaustion sets in and I'm left leaning against Soren for support.

But they haven't finished yet. And it's clear from their heavy breathing as Soren lays me on my back that they're just as much in need of satisfaction as I was.

I unroll their condoms, stroking Ash while I take Soren into my mouth, then switching things up after a few tentative licks. Back-and-forth I go, stroking one while sucking the other, until Soren buries himself deep against the back of my throat and fills my mouth with his salty tang.

As soon as he's finished, I release him, swallowing before doing the same for Ash. "So fucking hot," he groans before emptying himself.

He's right. It was hot — unreal, like a fantasy come true. And once the lusty haze clears, I don't feel the same immediate rush of guilt that I normally do. I'm tired of feeling like I have to apologize for what I want.

What I do know for sure is I should go before we end up doing that again. Not that I would complain, but I'm not sure how much more my body can take. If there's one thing they've proven, it's how ready they are to get naked at the drop of a hat. I don't trust myself around them.

Neither of them utters a complaint as I pull myself together, gathering my things and wrapping my wet suit in a towel before jamming it into my bag. My legs are still shaking by the time I place it over my shoulder and hug them both by the front door. "I'll see you guys at the arena on Monday. And remember —"

"Don't tell anybody," they respond in unison, snickering. I know better than to argue, so I only shake my head before heading outside. It's dark now, and quiet in this neighborhood. Oh, crap. We weren't loud enough for the neighbors to hear, where are we?

That's not even anywhere close to my biggest concern, revealed to me when I check my phone after getting in the car. The alert on the home screen makes my stomach drop.

Coach Kozak — 3 messages.

No. No, no, this isn't happening. Ryder wouldn't do this, would he? He wouldn't go to the coach and spill his guts.

But how many times has the coach reached out to me after hours?

He sent all three messages within seconds of each other.

Coach: we have a problem

Coach: I need to see you ASAP

Coach: tonight, if possible

And I was feeling so good about myself, too. Now I'm so nervous I can barely remember how to start my car, dreading whatever it is Coach Kozak has in store.

Knowing deep down inside that I'm already well aware.

Ryder finally decided to break his silence.

5

HARLOW

This is it. This is when all of my mistakes come back to bite me. I am still quivering in the aftermath of the strongest orgasm I can remember having in my entire life as I make my way from my car to the employee entrance. What had felt like a comfortable, balmy night when I left Ash's house has turned ominously cold, at least according to my overworked imagination.

It's amazing, really, how many ugly scenarios can run through a person's head in roughly twenty minutes. I'm ready for anything ranging from a scolding to getting fired outright by the time I enter the building, my flip-flops slapping the tile floor. The sound echoes all around me, adding to my overall dread.

It'll be okay. Whatever happens, you'll be fine. Sure, that's what I want to believe. I have a sneaking suspicion reality is not going to be that simple.

There's no firing squad waiting for me, and I'll take that as a good sign. The coach's office door is open, and from the looks of it, he is the only one left in the building besides the janitors. My heart's in my throat and I'm shaking so hard I can barely lift my hand to knock on the door frame.

When I manage to do it, his head pops up from behind his computer screen, and the sight of his angry scowl turns my stomach. "You wanted to see me?" I whisper.

He nods toward the chair on the other side of the desk. "Have a seat." He runs his hands through his gray hair, sighing heavily. Oh, this is it. He's never going to see me the way he used to. He won't respect me anymore – none of them will. I can't believe all my hard work has come to this. What was I even thinking earlier? Acting like I was some sex goddess calling the shots, putting my pleasure first. My desires. Look where it got me.

I lower myself into the chair, and it's good thing because my legs are so weak. I'm afraid they won't hold me up much longer. "What's the problem?"

He leans back in his chair, pinching the bridge of his nose between his thumb and forefinger and wincing like he's in genuine pain. Is that because of me, or because he's been squinting at his screen for so long? "Something's not working in the second line."

Hang on a second. I blink, waiting for more, but that's all he offers. "The second line?"

"As soon as we switch from first to second line, the intensity of our defense drops like a rock. I've been watching footage for hours, and it's always the same. I know we decided to move Ryder to the front line, but I'm wondering if it would be better to move him back to the second line instead."

He's talking, but my brain can't keep up with him. This is what he's so worried about? Sure, it's a problem, but did it need to be handled in a late-night meeting after three urgent messages?

If this is the worst I hear tonight, I'm lucky, and that's why I hold all of that in my head rather than asking why this couldn't have waited until Monday. I can sit up a little straighter now, though I'm still trembling thanks to the adrenaline that's been coursing through my system ever since I saw my phone. I need to get my head in the game here.

"The second line," I muse — and just like that, a new challenge slaps me in the face. "Ash and Soren are in our second line, aren't they?"

"Right, and the three of them have always played so well together."

Somebody up there is laughing at me. At this point, that's the only explanation I can come up with for this insanity. Just when I think I've avoided catastrophe, it sneaks up behind me. "We do still have that issue with Ryder and Ash to deal with."

"Did you manage to talk to either of them about it?"

Thinking fast, I shake my head. "I planned on meeting with Ryder, though. It sort of seemed like the aggression was coming from him rather than Ash, so I thought I'd get his side of things first."

"Right, of course. That makes the most sense. It can't be anything that serious, can it? You've spent time with these guys. What do you think?"

What a choice of words. "I think there's probably a lot they're not telling me, still," I venture. "I mean, there're plenty of things that go on in the locker room and during practice that I'm not present for. Who knows? It could be something as unimportant as a joke that landed the wrong way. The guys are always busting each other's balls, after all."

The hope that lights up his eyes both warms and chills me. He wants so much for that to be true. "Sometimes they don't know when to leave well enough alone."

"But I will meet with him tomorrow, and I'll try to get things straightened out. If it's anything super serious, I can always let you know."

"Do that. I have nothing but faith in you." Suddenly he blinks, and his head snaps back a little like he's seeing me for the first time. "I'm sorry. Did I pull you away from something?"

"What makes you ask that?"

"Your hair is damp. And you smell like chlorine."

"I was at a pool party." Was I ever. "But it's fine. I was on my way home when I got your messages."

"You'll have to forgive me," he sighs. "And don't take me seriously. This could've waited until Monday. I didn't mean to make you come in late on Friday. If I ever send you messages like that from now on, just know it can wait."

"I'll keep that in mind." Really, I'm so happy that I've been granted a stay of execution, it doesn't even matter anymore. And I doubt I could've waited until morning, considering how sure I was that I was about to lose my job. No way would I have gotten a wink of sleep tonight. I've always been the kind of person who would rather rip the Band-Aid off all at once.

It's only when I'm back in the car that the weight of what I've taken on my shoulders settles over me. I have to smooth things over with Ryder, obviously. If there's any hope of him playing on the same line as Ash and Soren, they'll have to find a way to coexist peacefully.

And I'm going to have to be the one leading the charge.

6

HARLOW

There are a lot of things I would rather do than drive to Ryder's house on a Saturday morning. A root canal sounds like a nice idea. Maybe a bikini wax. Or a trip to the accountant to have my taxes done. Really, I'm not picky.

But this? When I know how unhappy he's going to be?

Well, there's no sense in running away from the facts. That doesn't change anything. And it's not like I haven't given him plenty of time to try to get his thoughts together – I didn't push him or rush him into anything. But let's be honest, I did that just as much for myself as I did for him. Because once again, I am not looking forward to this.

The little script I came up with during a long, stressful night full of broken sleep and ugly dreams runs through my head as I navigate unfamiliar roads. *Things are complicated. The team is what matters. It's not worth risking your dream. I care about you as a friend.*

It's all fine and good to repeat these things to myself, but there's one key component missing from my little rehearsal, Ryder's reactions. I don't know if he'll even want to hear anything I have to say. I have to accept that, as much as I would rather everything go exactly the way I want it to. I mean, is that too much to ask?

I snicker at myself, shaking my head. If there's one thing I should know by now, it's that you can't have your cake and eat it, too. No matter how hungry you are or how good that cake looks.

Ash learned that today when we were on the phone. I called Soren first, knowing he would probably take the conversation better than Ash would. After I did my fair share of worrying about talking to Ryder, the next logical concern was what to do about those two. It's amazing how honest you can get with yourself in the middle of the night. I was too tired to soothe myself with any well-intended fairytales.

Facts are facts. I like both of them very much. It's pointless to pretend there's a world where we can coexist without ever giving in to the unreal chemistry we share. Telling myself otherwise is a waste of time — I mean, look where it's gotten me so far. How many times do I need to go back on a promise to myself before I stop making those pointless promises?

"If friends with benefits is the best I can hope for, then I guess that's what we'll be." I pretended not to hear the disappointment in Ash's voice. It's better for both of us that way. I'm not deluded. I knew he wouldn't be happy. Like me, he wants to have his cake and eat it too and I can't pretend not to know how that feels, no matter how tasty the cake is or how much fun it is to eat it.

I had to remind him once again what's at stake for me. How I am completely screwed if anybody ever finds out we're together. How it's much safer for us to be friends with benefits – discreet, careful, quiet – than to try to be anything more than that. Otherwise, I'm risking my job, my license, my future. Who would want to hire me? He finally seemed to get the point after that, and his attitude changed until he sounded a little more chipper. I knew that was the best I could hope for, so we left it there.

Now I'm left trying to find my way to Ryder's house in La Quinta. I don't even know for sure that he'll be home, but something tells me he wouldn't bother answering if I called to check. I can only hope that all the time that's passed since he walked in on the three of us has softened his memory from the day — though the opposite could just as easily be true. His wide-eyed surprise could easily have turned to bitter resentment by now. Even hatred for me, for the guys, maybe even for himself.

I hope that's not true. He deserves better than that. I'll be lucky if he even wants to hear a word I say, so I have to get as much of it out as I can right away, before he can slam the door in my face or shut me out.

It's late morning by the time I pull up to a beautifully landscaped entrance with a tall gate embedded in walls so white, they're almost blinding in the bright sunshine. Colorful flowers dot the grounds and a small fountain shoots jets of water that sparkle like diamonds before crashing down.

Ryder lives here? It makes sense — he would want something beautiful, even pristine, after spending so much of his early life fighting for whatever scraps he could get his hands on. Instead of a guard house, there's a keypad outside the gate. I made a note of the code for Ryder's house when I looked up his address on the team contact sheet. It's only a matter of typing it in and waiting to see if he'll answer.

All of a sudden, I hope he's not home. My insides are practically jelly, my legs are shaking, and everything I planned to say has left my head.

Just do it, already. I punch the code into the keypad before I can talk myself out of it.

"Hello?" He sounds vague, confused, like he's not used to random visits.

"Ryder? It's Harlow."

There's a heart-stopping beat of silence before he grunts. "What?"

"Please," I plead before he can disconnect us. "We need to talk. It's about the team."

"Go away."

There's knowing he'll be upset, and hearing it. Two totally different things. "It's important."

"Lots of things are important."

"Please, Ryder. I really need to speak with you."

"As a doctor?"

"As your friend."

He barks out a laugh that makes me flinch. "My friend? Oh, we're friends now."

"I want us to be. I always did."

"You have a funny way of showing it."

"I know you're mad, and you have every right to be."

"Thanks a lot. I'm glad I have your permission."

This is ridiculous. I'm leaning out through the car window, shouting into a speaker. And it doesn't help that there's another car pulling in behind me. "Listen. Open the gate so we can talk, please. I won't take up much of your time. But it really is crucial that I see you."

"You're only doing this because it's your job."

He is bound and determined to put me through my paces, isn't he? I deserve it, I know I do, and that's what keeps me from blowing up in frustration. "I'm doing this because your future is involved, too. Or does that not matter anymore?"

The silence which follows my question gets heavier with every passing second. *Come on, you're smarter than this.* I know he's smarter than this. But some people will cut off their nose to spite their face. All I can do is hope he's not one of those people.

He doesn't answer in words. Instead, he answers in the buzz from the gate before it begins to swing open. I'm so grateful, I could cry, but there's no room for relief when I'm still not sure how he's going to respond once I'm in front of him.

All I can do is hit the gas and pull forward, preparing to embrace my fate no matter what it happens to be.

7

HARLOW

It's like I'm driving through an ad for the ideal community as I slowly make my way to Ryder's house.

The streets are wide, absolutely pristine. There's not so much as a bottle cap or a cigarette butt or even a discarded flier anywhere to be seen. The houses sit behind emerald green lawns, and they're all huge. After hearing all about square footage and property values from both Kyle and my mother, I have to estimate they're somewhere in the three-to-four thousand square-foot range. The word *serene* comes to mind. Peaceful. Quiet.

In the center of the community is an enormous clubhouse. From the street, I see what looks like tennis courts, a driving range, basketball courts. There's a faint smell of chlorine in the air, so I'm guessing there's a community pool, though that could be the scent from the pools all around. I would imagine most if not all of the houses feature them. Ryder mentioned his during one of our early sessions.

It makes sense, him living in a place like this. All the space, all this wealth and privilege. Not that he's wealthy, per se, but he makes good money, and can afford this lifestyle because of it. He's come a long way from the kid who had nothing of his own in his early days. The kid who had to wear equipment that was too big for him if he hoped to learn to play hockey.

And he did. And now, it's up to me to make sure he doesn't blow it. Sure, his choices are his own, but I already know him well enough to know how self-destructive he can be. I don't need him using me as an excuse to blow it. I doubt I could live with myself if he did.

This place is like a maze, and all I can do is be grateful for GPS once I find the house and pull to a stop at the front curb. Just like the other homes in the area, his is sleek and modern, with lots of huge windows set in a stone façade. Two stories, with a curved set of stairs leading up to the front door. There's a two-car garage at the end of a wide, flagstone driveway. I won't park there – something won't let me do it. Maybe it's knowing I'm not welcome here. I walk along the driveway instead, then up the sweeping stairs before reaching the covered patio. The windows are slightly tinted so I can't get a look at the inside of the house. For all I know, he could be standing there, waiting for me on the other side of the glass.

My hand is shaking a little as I raise it to knock on the door. One moment after another passes in silence, and my heart sinks a little further with each one. I knock again, gritting my teeth against the frustration that's starting to build in my gut. The least he can do is let me inside. It's already hot, no big surprise, and I could use some relief.

Finally, there's nothing to do but jam my arm against the doorbell. "I know you're home," I mutter, glaring through the window next to the door in case he is having a good time, watching me stand here like an idiot.

After another minute passes, there's no choice but to give up being polite. I try the doorknob – and roll my eyes when it turns freely. But at least it gives me a way out of the heat.

The entry hall is two stories, dark and cool despite the sunshine streaming in from the windows covering the entire front wall. I take a few grateful breaths while looking around, wondering where to go. There's a staircase ahead, but walking upstairs would seem like an invasion.

"Ryder?" I call out, and my voice echoes in the cavernous space. "Where are you?" Silence is the only response I get. He's not going to make this easy, not like I thought he would.

And I thought the neighborhood was immense and tough to navigate? This house is gigantic – at least three thousand square feet, I'd estimate, with two separate wings branching off from either side of the entry hall. I slowly pass a large, airy living room, an office, even a home gym before finally reaching the kitchen at the rear of the house. It opens up into a home theater, while the backyard sits beyond a wall made entirely of windows. He even has an outdoor kitchen — there's what looks like a grill and a fridge out there, covered by an awning. This house would be great for parties and barbecues. I wonder if he ever has any.

The slamming of the refrigerator door makes me jump a little. There he is, holding packs of lunch meat in one hand, and a bottle of mustard in the other. He's wearing nothing but a pair of loose pants that look like they could be pajamas. I wonder if this is what he wears on his days off as I examine his six pack.

The one thing that's pretty obvious is that he doesn't want me here. He won't even look at me as he takes the food to the gray granite counter atop the island positioned in front of the stove. Six burners, that stove, and beside it is a pizza oven. He actually has a pizza oven in his kitchen. What must that feel like for a kid who grew up bouncing with his trash bag of clothing from one crammed foster home to another?

The iciness of the room has nothing to do with air-conditioning. He works quickly, efficiently, and still without so much as glancing my way. I don't know what to say, how to lead into this. For all my experience, I'm still clueless. I shift my weight from one foot to the other, wishing he would say something to break the cold silence.

Once he's finished piling the bread with slice after slice of turkey and Swiss cheese, he places his palms on the counter and hangs his head, sighing heavily. "What do you want? To stand there and watch me make a sandwich? if you have something to say, say it so you can leave."

I have no right to be upset. I am not the wounded party here. No amount of reminding myself that I never promised him anything will get me off the hook.

I have to remember what I'm here for. "I came to talk to you about the team. Coach Kozak wants to move you to the second line. He thinks you would help the defense stay aggressive, since things seem to fall off too easily otherwise."

He makes me wait, taking a huge bite of his sandwich and chewing slowly, staring out the window to the backyard. I have no right to rush him, even if it's verging on infuriating, the way he keeps me waiting. I need to be careful. I can't afford to upset him and make him shut down completely.

"So that's why you're here? To talk about me playing the second line? This couldn't have waited until Monday?"

"It was important enough to the coach that he called me in late last night." Alright, that's not exactly true, but it's close enough. "And I told him I would talk it over with you. I figured what's the use of waiting? It would give you a couple of days to adjust to the idea before you head back into practice on Monday."

He takes another bite and makes me wait until he swallows. "Refresh my memory. Who is on the second line again?"

"You know who's on the second line, Ryder," I tell him with a sigh, slowly approaching the island like I'd approach a wounded, growling animal. "Can we have an honest conversation about this? I get it. You hate me. I don't even blame you for that. I wish you wouldn't but, this is the team we're talking about, not you and me. And I need to be sure you can work with those guys."

"Why wouldn't I be able to?" He turns to me, finally, and I almost wish he hadn't when he pins me in place with a cold, unforgiving stare. "You know why."

"And I'm sorry. You have no idea how sorry."

He only snorts, smirking. "I am," I insist, quietly but firmly. "I don't know how to get it through to you."

"Let me guess. You made another mistake?"

"I…" I can't look at him, that's what. I knew he would be cold and even dismissive, but I can't stand facing him when he looks at me that way. Like I'm nothing. Like I'm a disappointment.

He props his elbows on the counter, resting his chin on his closed fists. "Well?" he asks, arching an eyebrow. "Let's hear it. Let's hear your excuse this time. You've had long enough to come up with one, and I'm dying to find out what it is."

8

HARLOW

I hate feeling like there's a spotlight trained on me. I want to shrink under the weight of Ryder's scrutiny, but I can't let myself do that. I'm an adult. I made my choices. And I don't have to defend myself — no matter how much it feels like I do.

"I am sorry for the way things happened."

He blinks rapidly, tipping his head to the side. "Wow. You make it sound like it was all a big misunderstanding. The way I remember it, you told me in no uncertain terms how complicated things are, and how —"

"I remember."

"No." He stands up straight again, tightening his jaw. "You don't get to do that. I've done you the favor of keeping my distance so things didn't get any more complicated – I didn't want to lash out."

"Thank you?" I mean, what does he want? Applause? "I'm glad you didn't escalate things."

"Could you drop the formal speech, please? I feel like I'm talking to a textbook."

"What do you want me to say? I meant it when I said I was sorry. I am. You have no idea how much."

"Why? Because you don't wanna lose your job?"

"Of course, I don't want to lose my job. But I don't want to hurt you, either. That's the truth. Whether or not you believe it."

He snorts, wearing what I can only describe as a skeptical expression. "I guess I just want to know why we were a mistake, but what I saw you doing with them wasn't."

I know I walked into this situation, wanting to smooth things over and make everything better if I could. Now I need to be patient. But the man could make an angel consider swearing. "There's nothing going on between us, if that's what you want to know."

"Why do you have to lie?"

"I'm not lying!"

"Don't tell me I didn't see what I know I saw. I've got twenty/twenty vision, Harlow. I walked in on you being spit roasted by those two, and you have the nerve to walk into my house and tell me there's nothing happening?"

It takes real concentration to force myself to take a deep breath, rather than blowing up worse than I already have. I'm trembling by the time I whisper, "All I meant was, we're not together or anything like that. It's not like I'm in a relationship with either of them."

"Well, congratulations. So you just fuck for fun every once in a while? Is that supposed to make things better?"

"It's a very casual thing. Like a friends with benefits situation. But that's all there is to it. I don't have, you know, feelings for them."

"No," he mutters, staring down at the granite countertop. "Why would you have feelings?"

"That's not fair."

"Life's not fair. You should know how familiar I am with that."

"For what it's worth, I didn't even know they were hockey players when we first met. It was totally by chance. I didn't find out I was hired by the team until after our one-night stand." I don't owe him an explanation, yet somehow I feel compelled to offer one. "So yes, that was kind of weighing on me during the interactions I had with you."

He snorts. "Interactions? Is that what you call it?"

"You know what I'm trying to say. I already had that weighing on me, and I told myself I should be more careful."

"But you weren't. You didn't even lock the door," he scoffs. "I mean, come on. What's it called when you deliberately make a mistake?"

He ought to know, since I've accused him of that very thing. "Self-sabotage," I whisper. "But it wasn't like that. It's not like I planned to do it. It just… happened. And I know how pathetic that sounds, but it's as close to the truth as I can come. I do wish it hadn't happened that way, and I definitely wish you hadn't seen it."

"Of course. Wouldn't want to jeopardize your career."

I smack my palm against the counter between us before there's time to stop myself. He's pushing me dangerously close to my limits. "It's more than that. I'm not going to pretend my career doesn't matter, but I do like you. We have fun together, and you're a good person. I hate to think that I ruined our friendship."

His steely eyes threaten to pierce me. "I'm not sure what you want me to say. Am I supposed to tell you it's all okay? That I don't care? I wish I didn't."

Me, too. He has no idea how much. "And I wish I could explain why I couldn't help but do what I did again. Really." I can't tell if his problem is with me choosing them, so to speak, or the fact that I was with the both of them at the same time. I wish I could get a read on that.

"Have you ever had a threesome?" I blurt out.

My sudden question leaves him widening his eyes. "Sure. Of course I have. I'm from Boston."

I squint my eyes like I understand what that's supposed to mean. Maybe it's better if I don't ask. "So you've done the same thing."

"That's different."

"How? I met the two of them at a bar one night and they came home with me. I didn't know anything about them, and they didn't know anything about me. And it was too late to do anything about it by the time I was hired."

"It was still different. For one thing, mine was with two girls."

Seriously? All I can do is stare at him, waiting for him to realize what he just said. His face falls all at once as reality sinks in. "Oh. I guess that's sort of the same thing for you."

"Yeah, it is. And everything else aside, there's nothing wrong with me being with both of them at the same time."

"That's not the issue. Fuck." He runs his hands through his hair, growling.

So it is about his ego. It's not like I couldn't have guessed. Just like Ash's anger when he felt rejected, Ryder hates feeling like I chose them over him. I wish I could make him understand that from where I was standing, there was no actual choice in the matter. I did what my body told me to do. It felt natural, even if we could've been a lot smarter about it.

"This is all new to me, you know. I'm trying to figure out what to do and how to feel."

He snickers. "It sucks to be you."

"Please, don't do that. I want us to be able to work together. I don't want there to be any anger or hard feelings. We were making real progress, weren't we?"

"Yeah. I guess we were."

"And you're going to have to play alongside them. The coach is dead set on it. And he's right – you add the intensity that's missing otherwise. But you can't go around slamming Ash, or Soren, or anybody else into the boards."

"Whatever." He rolls his eyes.

"No, I mean it. Do you want to keep this beautiful house? It is beautiful, and your neighborhood is gorgeous, and everything is amazing. I don't want to see you lose that. I'm sure you don't, either. You don't have to hang out with the guys and be best buds, but you have to put all of this aside for the sake of yourself, and the team."

"Which do you care about more?"

"I don't want to see you lose what you've worked so hard for," I insist, choosing my words carefully. "In the end, I was hired to help the team level up. I can care about both things at once – and I have to."

"Yeah. I guess so." I get the feeling he's coming around, if grudgingly. I would expect nothing less from him.

"I want what's best for everybody. But I can't defend you to Coach Kozak if you get out there and start fights."

He holds his hands up, sighing in exasperation. Like he's the one with a right to be exasperated. "I get it, okay? You don't have to keep hammering me like this."

Maybe I wouldn't have to if he would give me some clue about how he's really feeling. It drives me crazy. I don't think I've ever had to work as hard for anyone's forgiveness. That's what I want more than anything, I realize. I want him to forgive me, but at the same time, I don't want to beg for it. I wasn't trying to hurt him, and it's not like we're in a relationship. I wasn't cheating on him. I belong to me, nobody else.

Still… I can't pretend I don't understand how rejected he must've felt, only one day after I told him in no uncertain terms that we couldn't see each other outside of work anymore.

"I need you to know I didn't choose them over you," I tell him. He flinches, but doesn't say anything right away. He wants to hear what else I have to say. "And I'm still trying to navigate all of this. I know it's my job to seem like I'm on top of things. Like I have everything under control. But honestly, this is all so new for me."

"I bet." Is it my imagination, is there a little bit of that familiar humor in his voice? He's not being snide anymore. Dare I hope?

I'm not sure how to bring this to a close. What am I hoping for here? What's the ideal outcome? "Are we alright?" I venture.

If there's one thing he's good at besides hockey, it's leaving a girl hanging. I wouldn't go so far as to think he's savoring my anxiety, but he certainly doesn't bother putting an end to it right away, either. Eventually he lifts a shoulder. "I guess so."

Why don't I believe him? "And can I trust you to keep this between us? Please, nobody can know what you saw. I could lose everything. And yeah, that would be totally on me. I understand that. But I've worked so hard to get here, and I really think the team has so much potential. Please. All I want is the chance to prove myself. And you can help with that by not saying anything to anybody."

He absorbs this, and I give him the space to do it. He has to know he's holding my life in his hands, right? And I know he's a decent person – I wouldn't like him if he weren't.

When he nods his head, I can breathe again. "Fine. You have my word. Nobody will know."

An enormous weight leaves my shoulders all at once. I have to resist the impulse to flop across the island in relief. "Thank you."

Shouldn't I know by now that nothing is that easy? "So," he adds with a familiar grin, "how about we go to dinner sometime?"

9

HARLOW

"Hi, Miss Harlow!"

At the sound of that young, chipper voice, I search the ice to find a few of the girls from Corey's skating class, waving happily. One by one they notice me taking my seat, and it's sort of nice knowing I've made a good impression on them.

"Are you skating with us?" Sasha calls out. I have to fight off the impulse to cringe, since the performance is for the kids to show off what they've learned. It would look pretty dumb for an adult to be out there with them.

"No, you all are the stars!" I call back, waving both hands before taking my seat along with the other spectators. I didn't expect there to be such a crowd here today, but then again, this isn't only an exhibition for the kids. Corey will be performing, too, and that alone is worth the price of admission as far as I'm concerned. Clearly, I'm not alone — I don't recognize most of the people taking their seats, telling me they're here for her and not for the kids.

In front of me, a woman turns around wearing a rueful grin. "I'm sorry. I tried to explain to her that this was just for the kids and not for grown-ups."

I wave it off, laughing. "It's okay. And kids are the best judge of character, aren't they? If they like me, I must've done something right."

"Oh, Sasha loves you," her mother insists. "She wants to be just like Miss Harlow when she grows up."

I didn't expect that. "I don't know. If she knew me better, she might feel differently," I say with a laugh. We share a laugh before she turns around to chat with her friend.

Oh, Sasha. Was I ever that innocent as a child? Sure I was. Kids don't have the first idea what grown-ups go through. And how, no matter how old you are, there are still plenty of opportunities to make mistakes and wish you could do things over.

Really, all things considered, I can't complain. In the week since my talk with Ryder, things have improved. At least, I haven't heard about any fights on or off the ice, so I'll take that as a good sign. I'm sure if Coach Kozak had any concerns, he would share them with me. Loudly. Probably late at night.

That doesn't mean all is well. For one thing, Ryder's dinner invite is still hanging between us. I probably shouldn't have laughed when he asked – it was one of those things I couldn't control, something that burst out of me, because I figured he was joking. How could he be serious, asking a question like that after what we had just discussed?

But he was serious. He meant it. Right away, I made sure he wasn't blackmailing me or anything. "I can't believe you would think that about me," he grumbled. "Like I'm going to spread rumors if you turn me down?"

I told him I would think about it, if only to get out of there before I had to do something drastic like smack him upside the head for being a complete idiot. Who wouldn't take his sudden invitation as an ultimatum?

And think about it, I have. Not that it's done me any good. I'm just as torn as ever.

At least Ash and Soren have made good on their promises. They've been perfect angels, respectful and cordial the way the rest of the team is. There haven't been any lingering looks, any winks or double entendres.

As glad as I am, I can't help feeling like I am constantly running around, putting out fires. As soon as one is under control, another one springs up.

It's almost a relief when the lights go down and Corey skates out onto the ice. I can stop thinking in favor of observing. She looks beautiful in a shimmering costume, the kind skaters wear in competitions. It's an ice blue color, and when she moves, she sparkles. There's even glitter in her dark, shining hair. I wonder if her boyfriend managed to make it — with his schedule being as crazy as it is, she had her doubts. I would hate to think of him missing out on something like this.

First, the kids perform, showing off their moves to rapturous applause. At least, applause comes from people who aren't holding phones up to record everything, but those parents shout their kid's names, and cheer them on just the same. Behind me, I hear one of the parents praising Corey for being such a great teacher. "She's so good with the kids, and she gives them so much confidence out there." I have to stop myself from turning around and bragging that she's my friend.

After a half hour or so, it's time for the older students to strut their stuff. I can understand now why Corey put me in the class with the beginners, since some of the lifts and jumps these kids manage to perform leave me gasping in amazement.

But it's her performance that's the standout — no big surprise there, with her experience. The swell of emotional music sets the tone, and I watch as she moves fluidly, gracefully, making it look as easy as walking down the street. Like she doesn't even have to try while she flies through the air like she weighs nothing. I know it took years of practice and training and discipline to make it look that effortless, but it's easy to get swept up in the moment and forget everything I know in favor of feeling something. I guess that's the point. To be transported in the face of so much beauty and talent.

By the time the music comes to a thundering finish and she stops in the center of the ice, her arms extended overhead, I jump up to my feet along with everybody else in the arena to give her a well-deserved ovation. She crosses her hands over her chest and bows, and I would swear there are tears sparkling in her eyes as she turns slowly to acknowledge her adoring audience.

Once she's off the ice and the lights come up, I waste no time heading back to the dressing room. "For you, superstar," I announce, handing her a bouquet of white roses with a big flourish. "You were incredible. Honestly, I think I stopped breathing when you hit that triple toe loop."

She drops into a chair in front of the mirror, her mouth falling open. "Listen to you!"

"Hey, just because I suck at skating doesn't mean I've never watched it on TV." Noticing the room being otherwise empty except for the two of us, I venture, "I guess Sean couldn't be here?"

It's like a cloud drifts over her face, and I wish I hadn't brought it up. She deserves to be happy after what she did out there. "Yeah, he got called in. What are you going to do? I'm sure the parents here will send me the video they took."

"You can watch it together later."

"That's the plan." She mimes wiping sweat from her forehead. "I'm just glad it's over. I forgot how nervous I can get before a performance."

"Nobody would ever have guessed you were anything but totally in control out there."

"Well, that is sort of the idea. You can't let people know you're nervous as hell." When I narrow my eyes, she shrugs. "It's been a long time since I've performed for a crowd, even one as relatively small as this. I couldn't help but wonder if I got a little rusty."

"There is not a speck of rust on you, girl."

She beams in relief. "Thanks. So, are you ready for your trip?"

Pucking Disaster

I have to give it to her. She's just as good at changing the subject as she is at skating. "I think so. I've never been to Seattle before."

"It will be a break from the heat, at least. Though I hope you don't mind it raining most of the time."

"Are you kidding? I would welcome a little gloomy weather. I never thought I'd be so excited about the possibility of having to wear a jacket at night."

"And how's Ryder been? Do you think he'll be okay at training camp?"

He's not even half the problem – but then she doesn't know that. I'll have a lot more to worry about than Ryder while the team practices at the facilities used by the Seattle Orcas. Being an expansion team, the Blackhawks have the opportunity to run their training camp at a much bigger, more expensive facility.

And I'll be there with them. In a city I've never visited before, trying to balance the time I spend with Soren and Ash and the time I spend with Ryder, who I doubt will let up with the pestering when it comes to whether or not we're going to dinner. "He asked me out, you know."

"He what? Why didn't you tell me?"

"You were so busy getting ready for the showcase."

She waves a dismissive hand, scowling. "That's kind of a big deal. What did you say?"

"I told him I'd think about it."

"He's not trying to pressure you, is he?"

"No." But there are other pressures. Like the pressure I felt when I noticed the smug little grin Ash shot at the back of Ryder's head when they were coming out of practice a few days ago. Ryder didn't notice – I might have been the only one who caught it, actually. I hope so. I can't help but wonder if Ash weren't secretly pleased that Ryder walked in, especially since he was so jealous in the first place when he found out we'd slept together.

"That's good. He seems like a nice guy, but there's no excuse for that."

"No, I'm sure it'll be fine."

"You are a terrible liar."

All I can do is groan while she giggles. "Tell me something I don't know."

"Don't forget to call me and fill me in on everything. But I'm telling you, if he doesn't stop pestering you, I will fly up there. Now that I have a break between classes, I would love nothing more than an excuse to take a trip."

"I thought you and Sean were going to spend all that time together, though." I wiggle my eyebrows up and down.

"Yeah, but you know how it is. There's never any guarantee he'll have free time, anyway." There's a wistfulness in her voice that goes straight to my heart. We're still not exactly what I'd call close, though we're getting there, and I wonder if she would confide in me if things were going badly between them.

A knock at the door interrupts before I can gently ask if there's anything she wants to talk about. "Miss Corey? Can my parents get a picture of us together?"

"Sure thing!" And then she does something I've never noticed before, but it makes perfect sense. She puts on a vibrant, glowing smile so suddenly, it's like somebody flipped a switch to take her from glum, frowning, and wistful to a woman without a care in the world. I guess, after spending years performing, you get used to putting on a happy face even if you don't necessarily feel that way.

And it makes me wonder how often she has to do it.

10

HARLOW

Boy. Am I glad I got an Uber for this.

"I almost took off your bumper!" My driver is not in a good mood, but then I wouldn't be, either. Traffic has been an absolute nightmare the entire way to the airport, but the true gauntlet is the airport itself. Cab drivers weave in and out, people cross without looking to make sure they won't get run over. We've come to so many sudden stops, I'm starting to get car sick. "What is it about airports that makes people think they can drive like total idiots?"

"You can let me out here, if you want," I offer in a small voice. I would like to make it to the plane in one piece.

"The terminal's just up ahead," he tells me, so all I can do is hope he doesn't fly into a rage between here and there.

The thing is, if I were driving, I wouldn't be dealing much better with the traffic around Palm Springs International. I'm nervous enough about this trip as it is. It's amazing I have any fingernails left after chewing them all morning.

"So where are you headed?" he asks when we come to a stop behind a van that's more like a clown car. How many people were crammed in there? They keep tumbling out with their bags, taking their time. *Relax, already.*

"Oh, I'm flying to Seattle."

"Wow, business or pleasure?"

"Business."

"What do you do?"

I normally don't love getting chatty with Uber drivers, but if anything, it's a distraction. "I am the sports therapist for the Palm Springs Blackhawks. We're heading up for training camp at the Orcas facilities."

"Wow, that's really interesting. Hell of a lot better than this gig."

"I'm sure you get to meet some interesting people."

He meets my gaze in the rear view mirror. "I had to convince a couple of passengers last night that it wasn't okay to give or receive a blow job in my car."

And now I look down at the seat, hoping he stopped them before they got started. "That's… unfortunate."

"Here's hoping you have a nice trip." He pulls to a stop outside the terminal and I thank him profusely before getting out and taking my bags from his trunk.

Just when I'm sure I can't stand the stress of my job, I'm reminded how much worse things could be.

This is my first time on a private plane. The entire team is flying together, along with their spouses, the staff, everybody. I hope there's no drama among certain teammates – I don't need anybody arguing over who is sitting where.

Normally, I wouldn't even consider it. I mean, I'm just me, I'm not worth fighting over. Still, I can't shake the memory of Ash's smirk at the back of Ryder's head. I would hate to see either of them start an argument.

After handing my luggage over to one of the airport personnel, I climb the stairs and board the plane. From the looks of it, I'm one of the last people to arrive. Considering the traffic situation, that's no big surprise. I wave and murmur greetings to the players as I walk down the center aisle, scanning the seats.

"Harlow! Back here." Coach Kozak waves from halfway back. I'm glad he wants me to sit with him, even if I would've liked to sit back with a book or a podcast during the flight. But if we are sitting together, nobody will approach me, at least not in an unprofessional way.

"This is very exciting." I stash my carry-on in the overhead compartment before sitting down and buckling my belt.

"Have you ever been to Seattle?"

I shake my head. "But I made sure to bring plenty of clothing options for the weather."

"It's a big change from Palm Springs." Of course, he has his binder spread out on the table attached to the back of the seat in front of him. I can imagine him sleeping with that thing.

"I see you've been busy," I point out with a smile.

"When am I not?" He looks around over the tops of the seats, wearing a fond smile as he does. In many ways he's like a proud parent. "But I have to tell you, there's one thing I'm not worried about at all."

"What's that?"

"The attitude around here. There's a lot more positivity now than there was at the end of last season."

The way he says it makes me tingle to the ends of my hair. "Do you think so?" At the end of the day, I'll always be the girl looking for a gold star on her test. This is the biggest test I've ever taken.

"Don't get me wrong. The guys aren't walking around spouting off positive mantras or whatever they're called. But there's been a lot less bitching and whining, and a lot more asking how things can be improved. They're looking for solutions instead of looking for somebody to blame."

He elbows me, grinning. "You wouldn't happen to know why that is, would you?"

I can't help but blush. "I don't know. Maybe I have a little something to do with it."

"You have a lot to do with it, and don't think I haven't noticed. I might not praise you all the time, but I see the difference. Even Ryder turned things around this week. Moving him to the second line worked like a charm."

"I'm really glad." I'm also really fighting off the urge to squirm. Guilt is a funny thing. I can't take pleasure in being praised and appreciated, because I've been lying to this man from the beginning. Why should it be any different, I guess.

Suddenly, his bushy eyebrows grow together. "I wanted to give you a heads up. We might have some challenges ahead."

Whew. I've barely had time to absorb his praise, and now we're back to discussing challenges. I could get whiplash. "Like what?"

His eyes dart around like he's making sure nobody's listening in. "Some of the players will be on the receiving end of two-way contracts with the Orcas. But let's not spread that around just yet."

"Of course." I wonder which players will get called up. In some ways, that's a great thing – the opportunity to play in the NHL for a certain number of games. But once the games are up, the players go back to the team they came from. I wonder what kind of impact that will have on a player like Ash, getting a taste of the big leagues only to have it taken away again.

Coach's concerns are a little more immediate. "We're facing the prospect of some of our best players being away for what could be large periods of time."

"Right. That could have an effect on morale, not to mention how I'd imagine the players would have to scramble around to fill in the gaps."

"Exactly. As great as things are going now, there could be some minor chaos in the future."

Three players immediately come to mind. Our connection has nothing to do with it either. They're easily three of the best players, all of them with the potential to play a much bigger game.

What would the team look like without players like Ash, Ryder, and Soren? It wouldn't be permanent, but who's to say? The Orcas could decide to sign one of them permanently if they make a strong enough impression. Much stranger things have happened. I know that's what Ash wants, to be called up permanently. Play in the NHL for the rest of his career. I have no doubt every single player on this team would like that – even the older players for whom the opportunity has pretty much passed.

"I'll make a point of planning what to say and how to help them through it when the time comes," I offer. "And we can always make up a new scheme for restructuring the lines."

"I'd appreciate that." The door closes and applause rises up all around us. "Here we go. Next stop, Seattle."

I grin, giving him a thumbs up.

All the while, I can't help wondering whether I'll miss any of the guys while they're gone.

11

HARLOW

"I want to see! Turn the camera around so I can see the rest!"

I roll my eyes at Ruby but oblige her, tapping my screen so the camera faces the sliding door leading out to my balcony. Now she gets to admire the view the way I've been doing ever since we arrived at the hotel. It's gorgeous, like a completely different world from the one we left just hours ago. So lush, so mild. The sweet, cool air that slapped me in the face when I stepped out of the plane almost knocking me down the stairs. I was so pleasantly surprised.

"Wow," she marvels. "Everything is so green. And there's all that water!"

"We're right on the Sound. After living in the desert all this time, I don't know what to do with myself."

"What's the temperature like?"

"Oh, my God, it's fantastic. It's supposed to go into the low sixties tonight."

"I am so jealous."

"I would be jealous of me, too. I don't know if I would want to live here year-round," I admit. "Apparently it rains almost half the year."

"Oh, not cool."

"Still. I can see visiting here in summer, like now. It's so much more pleasant. I even managed to make it from the car to the lobby without sweating."

"That sounds miraculous." She settles back in her armchair, no longer admiring the scenery. "So. How are you going to handle this trip?"

"Meaning?" I ask, suspicious.

"You know what I mean. You're gonna be staying in the same hotel with men you've slept with. Men you continue to sleep with."

It's childish, but I look over my shoulder toward the door, just the same. What do I expect? To find out somebody came in without me noticing? "That's not going to be a problem."

She taps her chin, frowning. "Why do I feel like I've heard you say that numerous times?"

"Why am I even friends with you?"

"You said there's a king size bed in that room?"

"Ruby…" I warn, plopping down on that very bed. It's firm but still soft. I could easily close my eyes and drift off, though I guess my late night spent last-minute packing has something to do with that.

"Just saying. Plenty of room for you and anybody who would like to join in."

Fun is fun, but I'm starting to feel gross. "Do me a favor. Don't make it sound like I'm the team's blow-up doll."

She winces. "I didn't mean for it to sound that way," she murmurs, apologetic. "I'm only teasing."

"I know." I'm irritated because I've wondered these exact same things. How much more awkward it could get thanks to the fact that all four of us are now under the same, giant roof. "All I can do is hope the guys will be careful. I don't need the coach seeing any of them sneaking in here, or hanging around the door trying to get me to answer."

"You just need to set boundaries." She makes it sound so easy. Like all I have to do is snap my fingers, and the three of them will behave. All of them have proven more than once how disinterested they are in playing it safe. Even for my sake.

This is a new day. A new situation. I guess I have to have a little faith.

Once we're off the phone, I change out of my comfy travel clothes in favor of putting on a sundress and sandals. It's cute, informal, but still nice enough that I could get away with wearing it to dinner if I decide to go out later. So far, the only plans I've made involve meeting up downstairs in the hotel bar, but I would like to keep my options open.

There's a noise down in the courtyard, loud enough to travel up to my room. I open the sliding door to step onto the balcony, then immediately start rubbing my arms to ward off the chill. After acclimating to the weather in Palm Springs, it might as will be winter as far as my body is concerned.

Peering over the edge of the railing, I see a wedding party stepping out of a handful of limos, while people standing all around applaud and wish them well. It's sweet, and it makes me smile, but it's also chilly as hell so I scurry back inside and close the door. Maybe the sundress wasn't a great idea. I did bring cardigans and even a jacket, so I settle on a light sweater and hope for the best.

Down in the bar, there are already around a dozen players drinking beers and watching a Mariners game on the TV. "Hey, Doc! Buy you a beer?" Max calls out, waving me over.

"And what would your wife think about you buy me a beer?" I tease, laughing when he blushes a little. "I'm only kidding. I would love one. Where is she, by the way?" I ask, looking around and finding myself the only woman here.

"She's upstairs getting fixed up. We're heading out to dinner."

"Watch out," Danny warns, smirking. "Don't let the coach know you're going out."

"Why not?" I ask.

"He'll make a big deal about getting sleep before the first practice tomorrow."

Max laughs knowingly as he hands me a pint glass from the bartender. "Yeah, well, he can talk that out with Heather. She went through all the trouble of having her parents watch the kids while we're gone, and she's going to want at least one dinner out."

"Yeah, he's a tough guy, but I wouldn't want to see him up against an angry wife." We all laugh together and chat some more while the bar continues filling up with various players wandering in after unpacking in their rooms. The bar gets pretty crowded, in fact so much so that the bartender has to hustle to keep up with the orders flooding in.

"Have you ever been to Seattle?" Danny asks.

I shake my head. "This is my first time. I can't wait to take a look around."

"If Coach gives you a minute to yourself," he jokes. "He's starting to rely on you about as much as he relies on that binder of his."

Max lets out a belly laugh, "Did anybody ever tell you about the time a rookie hid it from him?"

"No!" I'm darn near horrified at the idea.

"One of the older guys — he's not on the team anymore — convinced him to do it. Just an innocent prank, you know." He grimaces while rubbing the back of his neck. "That was a dark day."

"I hid in the locker room," Danny admits. "It was safer."

"That's such a shame. He must've been half out of his mind."

Max nods. "That's one way to describe it." Suddenly his eyes light up, his attention darting over my shoulder. It's like magic, the change that comes over him. And I know why, without being told.

Sure enough, when I look over my shoulder to see what he's staring at, I find a pretty, petite brunette elbowing her way through the crowd. "I'm surprised I could find you!" she laughs, fanning herself. "Did you all decide to come down here and drink at the same time?"

Pucking Disaster

"Why not?" Danny asks. Heather is not alone, either – a few of the other wives I met on the way here link arms with their husbands and pull them away, looking to have a nice night together before training camp starts.

How funny. There's a strange sort of empty feeling in my chest once I wave them off and return my attention to the ballgame. Not like I was really paying attention, but now there are fewer people to talk to.

Seeing the way Max reacted to Heather's entrance must've been what brought me down. I can't remember a single time when Kyle reacted that way at the sight of me. I wonder if anyone ever will. Here I am, playing around, enjoying myself, but with no strings attached. I figured I'd be engaged by now, planning my wedding, but I'm as single as I've ever been.

Slowly, the bar empties out, the boisterous chatter fading to quiet conversation. I'm finishing my second beer and considering ordering something to eat when I realize the situation I'm in now.

In the mirror behind the bar, I catch the reflection of the last three players left behind. Ash and Soren are to my left, at the other end of the long bar, while Ryder sits three stools down on my right.

How the hell did this happen? Considering Ash and Soren keep shooting glances over my head to where Ryder is nursing a beer, I'm going to guess they want to wait him out.

But I know Ryder, too. He's a patient man when he wants to be.

And here I am in the middle, suddenly wondering if I should've stayed in my room, after all.

12

ASH

Well. Isn't this an interesting turn of events?

"Look who finally decided to pay attention." Soren finds this as funny as I do. There we were, making bets on how long it would take Harlow to notice we were the only ones left here in the bar. She was staring up at the TV, watching the game, but I get the feeling she was far away. She didn't even react when one of the Mariners hit a grand slam.

And here I am, wondering what that means. Wondering if she's upset, and if so, what has her feeling this way. Wishing I could go to her and ask if she's alright.

I don't know who I am anymore when it comes to her. When I'm not with her, I wish I was. When I am, I can't help myself. I have to touch her, kiss her, even when she puts on a front and tries to discourage me. She's never actually said no, never pushed me away in the moment. All that does is add fuel to the fire burning away inside me. A fire she set the night we met back in West Hollywood.

She looks adorable, too, in her cute little dress. The dress I would very much like to pull over her head and throw into a corner. I doubt she has the first clue how tempting she is, just like I'm sure she doesn't set out to be. Maybe I am a hopeless addict who can't help the way my thoughts travel in that direction.

Meanwhile, there's Ryder, brooding as always. It's like he decided to make it his life's mission to be moody and miserable. His shoulders are hunched up around his ears as he practically hovers over his beer, like he's trying to protect it. He won't look over here. That's probably for the best, since I might have no choice but to wink or grin if he did. I don't think Coach Kozak would appreciate a fistfight in the bar.

I might be an asshole, but I'm not that big of an asshole. I know how little it takes to push him over the edge when he's good and pissed, and there's not a doubt in my mind how mad he is right now. Or how mad he could be if I gave him an excuse.

Harlow stares down into her empty pint glass, turning it in slow circles while chewing her lip. What is she thinking? What is she going to do? I hope she doesn't chicken out and run back to her room. It's been more than a week since the last time we were together at my house. I could use a hit of my drug of choice.

"So, looking forward to the start of training camp?"

Soren snorts beside me at Harlow's question. "What a lead-in," he murmurs, snorting again. Rather than look at any of us, she watches us in the mirror behind the bar, her gaze darting back-and-forth. The way her brows draw together and the almost pained pinching of her lips softens my attitude a lot. She's really nervous. Uncomfortable. Maybe this isn't so funny, after all. I don't like thinking of her in genuine pain or discomfort because of us.

Then there's the other part of me that wants to know here and now what she feels for him. Sue me. I'm only human. And I still can't get over the fact that she slept with him after she was with us. What, were we not good enough? It sure seems like we were the last time she screamed like a banshee while riding my dick.

Ryder finally acknowledges us, shooting me a dirty look before doing the same to Soren. What is he thinking? Is he remembering how it felt to walk in on us in her office? Again, sue me. I can't help the rush of satisfaction that moves through me when I remember the look on his face. He figured out he's not the only man she's interested in. He's not that special, after all.

And knowing the size of his ego, it had to be a knife to the chest.

"I think it'll be fun," I announce. "New scenery, new facilities."

"Yeah," Soren agrees. "Sometimes you need to try something new. I like having a break in the monotony. It makes life more interesting." He's barely concealing his laughter.

"Seriously?" Ryder turns his body on the stool until he's facing us, craning his neck to look around the back of Harlow's head. "That's not what we need to be talking about. We're wasting time here."

The balls on this guy. And the way he sounds, too. Like a jealous boyfriend. Like he has any claim on her. Right away irritation blooms in my chest, and it's not long before I'm dangerously close to venting it in the form of a few not-so-carefully chosen words.

Soren's too quick for me. "Gee, Ryder," he replies in an innocent voice that's anything but. "Exactly what do you think we should be talking about, then? We are here in Seattle for training camp. Should we discuss this year's orange harvest in Florida? Or maybe the heat wave in Texas?"

"Laugh all you want." He glances Harlow's way, and it could be the dim lighting in here messing with my perception, but I swear he flinches a little when he finds her staring straight ahead. The girl wishes she could disappear. I feel it. I understand her.

I like her way too much. I think about her too much, I care too much what she thinks and feels.

And let Soren dick around all he wants, but I know him, too. He feels the same way.

"Fine, man," I tell him. "Do you want to start shit? I mean, we're sitting here like normal people, having a good time, but you want to make something out of it. By all means. Cause a scene."

"Do not cause a scene." Harlow's voice is sharp as the crack of a whip. Sharp enough to silence the three of us. She swivels on her stool, eyes blazing, and I have never so much wanted to throw a woman over my shoulder and run off with her as I do right now. I can hardly breathe.

She glares at Ryder until he averts his gaze, suddenly interested in the floor. My satisfaction is short-lived, though, because she turns that penetrative stare on me next. "This is ridiculous," she tells us in a fierce whisper. "We are all adults. All of this sulking and egging each other on is immature, and beneath you."

"He started it." *Oh, way to go, Ash. That's not immature at all.*

"Do I care? No. I do not." She folds her arms, huffing, her face going red. "I'm disappointed in all of you. And honestly, that's not what we're here for. You have the opportunity to prepare for the season, and all you want to do is bicker?"

"I wasn't trying to bicker. I want to have a conversation." It's amazing anything Ryder says is intelligible, considering how tightly his jaw is clenched.

"That was a hell of a way to lead into a friendly conversation," Soren mutters. He's not kidding around anymore, either. That's the thing about him. He's lighthearted and easygoing until he's not. Once that happens, you're pretty much up shit creek.

"Enough. All of you. This is just silly." Her gaze swings back and forth. "Can't you just get along? I thought things were going better."

"I can play nice during practice," Ryder grunts.

My head snaps back. "And what is that supposed to mean? Are you going to try to kick my ass now that we're here at the hotel?"

Harlow makes a move like she's ready to get up and stand between us, but something cuts her off.

No. Someone.

"Alright." The coach follows that up by briskly clapping his hands as he enters the room. "Let's go. Clear the bar."

Harlow swings back around, facing the TV. Ryder stands down, shoving his hands into his pockets while his posture relaxes like we were only having a friendly conversation.

"It's still pretty early, Coach," I point out.

"I don't wanna hear about it. Do you want to eat? Get room service. No going out, no staying down here. First practice is at seven sharp, and you'd all better be on your game. No excuses."

I nod, holding my hands up in surrender. "Fair enough. We'll see you in the morning." I toss a few bills onto the bar and so does Soren, but I'm not in any hurry. I want Ryder to leave first.

After a few heavy moments, he pulls his wallet from his back pocket and withdraws a few bills for the bartender before skulking away.

But then, to my dismay, Harlow follows him, practically fleeing the room. Coach catches up with her, though, and asks her a question as they leave. My relief is palpable. As long as I know she's not chasing after Ryder, it's fine. I can rest easy.

"He's going to be a problem," Soren muses as we leave the bar.

"Going to be?" I ask. "It looks like he already is."

13

HARLOW

"I'll see you in the morning. Have a good night." I step off the elevator when it stops on my floor and offer the coach a little wave before the doors close to take him up another floor.

Only once the doors are closed between us can I release some of the tension that's spread throughout me from head to toe. What a complete mess. I'm not sure who I'm more annoyed with among the three of them. Ryder didn't have to start things in the first place, but then Soren's sarcastic attitude didn't help. Then there's Ash, egging him on.

And there I was, stuck in the middle.

It's a relief to reach my room, to close the door on everything else. I lean against it, heave an exhausted sigh, and close my eyes. What am I going to do with these guys? I was pretty naïve to think things were actually better with Ryder. He made a good point down there, just because he didn't get into any fights during a scrimmage doesn't mean everything's hunky-dory. I'm proud of him for doing the right thing for the sake of the team, but I guess that only extends to team activities. Once they're outside the arena, it's no holds barred.

If it hadn't been for Coach coming in when he did, I'm afraid things would have gotten much worse. The bartender looked like he was ready to ask us to leave. Talk about uncomfortable. Word would've gotten back to Coach Kozak, no doubt, and how would I have explained things?

What am I going to do? Sure, it's good to know Ryder won't start trouble in front of the coach or anybody else involved with the team. He has been true to his promise of keeping our secret to himself.

But it would be wrong of me to dismiss what comes along with that. He's still hurt, and that hurt is coming through in the form of anger. Ash certainly isn't helping any by making little digs and escalating the situation. Soren's sarcasm is the icing on the poison cake.

Because of me? I can hardly wrap my head around the idea. These men are fighting because of me. Sure, there's more than a healthy dose of ego in the mix, but still. It all started because I slept with them.

As far as I understood, they were friends before I entered the picture.

Am I really worth all this? I can't imagine it.

Pushing away from the door, I walk to the other side of the room, gazing out at the Sound in the distance and wondering how I'm supposed to navigate any of this. Should I have stuck up for Ryder somehow? No. That would've made things worse. It was better for me to stay quiet until I couldn't stay quiet anymore.

And let's face it. That would've been the same as approving of his behavior. He was the one being petulant and confrontational in the first place.

He looked so angry and hurt as he was leaving the bar, too. I hate to think of him being alone in his room, brooding, maybe wondering if I went off with Soren and Ash. I know it isn't my responsibility to protect his feelings, but I'm not heartless. He's a good person, and he obviously hasn't gotten over feeling wounded and betrayed.

How would I handle this if he were nothing more than a friend? If there were no history between us, brief as it was?

I would reach out to him. I would offer to listen if he wants to vent. I would try to pick up his spirits. I mean, that's what I would do for Ruby. Why does it have to be any different just because he's a man? If I want to get us past this ugly patch and move on to a place where we can coexist peacefully, like friends, I have to treat him like one. Not like the guy I regret sleeping with. Not like the guy whose heart I might have dented a little.

We never did have that dinner, did we?

Is this the worst idea I've ever had? It could very well be. But I won't be able to rest tonight if I don't at least make the effort to reach out and smooth things over. Not for Soren. Not for Ash. Not even for the team.

For myself. For Ryder.

I pick up my phone and pull up our text chain. I have to cringe at the visual reminder of how one-sided things have been lately — there was a point where he texted me several times a day, right after we slept together. That was only a couple of weeks ago, right? How does it feel like half a lifetime has passed?

Before I can stop myself, I type out a quick message.

Me: Still interested in having dinner? I never ate. Did you?

Now, there's nothing to do but pace at the foot of the bed like a caged animal, wringing my hands, biting my nails. I wonder if it's possible to wear a hole in the carpet with all this back-and-forth. One minute passes, then another, while the phone sits dark and silent on the bed. I have to fight the urge to send another message full of apologies and pleas for him to forgive me. I've always hated conflict. I'm sure my childhood has a lot to do with that.

Come on, man. This is not the time for your pride to get in the way. I guess if he doesn't bother answering, I'll have to accept that. This is all supposed to be for his sake, anyway. To let him know I care. I don't think what he started downstairs was cool, and I'll let him know how I feel, but I don't think it was okay for the guys to be snarky and sarcastic, either.

At least five minutes pass before the phone buzzes, and I jump on it like it's a live grenade.

Ryder: No, I didn't eat yet. But you heard the coach. No going out.

Me: I was thinking more along the lines of raiding the minibar. Maybe a drink and a pack of M&Ms?

Hopefully he takes that in the spirit it was intended. We had so much fun together at first, didn't we? At that little greasy spoon diner, where we ate burgers and fries and I probably told him way too much about my family life and how I grew up. I couldn't help it. He's so easy to talk to, and he seemed genuinely interested. It had been a long time since I sat down with a man and he encouraged me to talk about myself. Kyle certainly never did.

I had no idea how needy I could be until now. Don't they say every bad situation is really a life lesson? If so, these past several weeks have been the equivalent of a master's degree in myself.

The phone buzzes again, signaling the arrival of a four-word response.

Ryder: I don't think so.

My dismayed gasp echoes in the room. Damn. I didn't expect that. It was stupid of me not to — here I go, assuming things. I don't blame him one bit for wanting to be alone.

But it hurts. He really hates me. I thought we could work our way through this.

Ryder: I'm going to need to order from room service. A pack of M&Ms isn't going to do it.

Oh, for fuck's sake.

I fall back onto the bed, groaning. Way to give me a heart attack. Once I stop inexplicably shaking, I send my response.

Me: Sounds good. I'm in room 512.

The second I send it off, one thought rings out loud and clear in my head.

I sincerely hope this isn't a mistake.

14

HARLOW

"Thank you very much." I hang up the phone and blow out a sigh. The girl downstairs told me it would be fifteen to twenty minutes before the food arrives. I shoot Ryder a text to let him know.

Ryder: Sounds good. I'll be down in a little bit.

Okay…and then what?

Nobody has to ask my body that question. The blooming of heat between my thighs is enough. There goes Pavlov's dog again, sitting up and salivating at the idea of being in the same hotel room as this man.

I doubt it would be that easy with him, anyway. He's not going to be in the mood to forget everything else and fall into bed. We do need to have a talk. This can't devolve into a physical situation before we talk about his feelings. He's still carrying a chip on his shoulder, roughly the size of an iceberg — and like an iceberg, there's a lot more going on under the surface. He can put on a decent show during practice, acting like everything's okay. That says a lot for his maturity, not to mention his sense of responsibility toward the team.

How long before he can't do it anymore? If all he does is push his feelings deep down to get through working alongside the two men I'm sleeping with, his resentment is going to eat away at him like rust. Eventually it will wear a hole, and that's when all hell is going to break loose. Better to settle things now if we can.

Goosebumps cover my arms, and I rub them briskly, distracted as I look over the room to make sure there's nothing embarrassing sitting out in the open.

That's when I realize I'm not wearing my sweater anymore.

I bought it downstairs, didn't I? What did I do with it? My heart sinks when I remember taking it off when things got a little too crowded down there. I draped it over the back of my stool, but I was in such a hurry to get the hell out of there that I completely forgot it. Great.

There's plenty of time to rush down and grab it. I don't want to miss the room service delivery, but it only takes a few minutes to get down to that level, and the bar isn't far from the lobby. I make sure I've got my room key before ducking out, then hurrying down to the elevator. Considering Ryder ordered half the menu, I'm sure it's going to take a while to put everything together, anyway.

Some of the members of the bridal party I noticed earlier have trickled into the bar from the ballroom on the other side of the hotel. No big surprise, my sweater is nowhere to be found now. But when the bartender notices me, he holds up a hand to get my attention. "Here. I noticed it when you left." He reaches underneath the bar and hands me a neatly folded cardigan.

"Thank you so much — and I'm sorry if things got a little tense earlier," I add. None of that was my fault, and it's not like a fight broke out or anything, so why do I feel like I have to apologize? Ever the good girl, never wanting to rock the boat.

He only snickers, waving it off. "No big deal. You don't know half of what I've dealt with around here."

I'm sure he's got plenty of stories to tell. People tend to leave their manners at home when they go away for a vacation, conference, whatever. Even now, a guy in a tuxedo and a girl in what has to be a bridesmaid's dress are making out sloppily at the end of the bar. He's about to slide his hand inside her dress by the time I turn away, ready to rush back upstairs.

The big, airy lobby is full of life. People coming and going, wandering back in from dinner or heading out for a late night. More than a few of them walk hand-in-hand or with their arms around each other's waists. It's sweet. I wonder if they know how lucky they are.

"Hey, you."

The sound of a familiar voice startles me. It doesn't take much looking to find Ash coming my way. I don't know what he's doing down here. I only know he's maybe the last person I need to deal with at this particular moment. The clock is ticking, my food will arrive soon… And Ryder will be on his way, too.

"Hey. What's up?" I crane my neck to look behind him. "Where is your other half? I almost never see one of you without the other."

His head snaps back like he's startled, or maybe just insulted. "He's up in his room, I guess."

"Shouldn't you be in your room?" I fold my arms and raise an eyebrow. "You heard what Coach said."

"Listen to you." When I don't smile back, his brows draw together. "I didn't know we were on lockdown."

"You're not. I'm only kidding. I came down to grab my sweater." I hold it up like there's any need to prove myself. "I'm on my way back to my room."

"Can I join you? I was hoping we could —"

"I have a feeling I know what you were hoping we could do. Really, though, I would like to get some rest." I slide past him, headed for the elevator, and for some reason my heart is pounding. Maybe because I don't like being rude, and I feel like I'm being rude right now. Trying to dodge him, being dishonest.

At the same time, he is going out of his way to be obtuse, following me even when I've made it pretty clear I want to be alone. "To talk. I was hoping we could talk."

"And I'm hoping for a million bucks to magically appear in my bank account." I feel bad for saying that, so I look over my shoulder before coming to a stop in front of the closed elevator doors. "Sorry. But I really do want to get some rest before tomorrow. We can talk about things, but not tonight, okay?"

I'm hoping that's it as I step into the car. Silly me. Well, he needs to get to his room, I guess. I can't bar him from the elevator.

"You sure you want to be alone?"

The playful tone in his voice sets my teeth on edge. "Ash, I'm not in the mood for this. I know what I want." Why can't this elevator move any faster?

"Funny, because you've swung back and forth in the past."

"Not funny."

"But it's the truth. Sometimes the truth isn't funny."

"Fine. Do you want to hear the truth? It's not so much that I want to be alone as it is that I don't feel like going through the same song and dance tonight. That's the truth. And I really hope you don't think we're going to spend all our time in Seattle with you following me to my room."

His eyes flash dangerously, sending a shiver down my spine. "I was sort of hoping you would invite me."

"Not tonight. You need rest more than I do. Coach is going to put you through your paces tomorrow."

The doors open with a soft chime, and I barely wait until there's enough space for me to step out into the hall.

Except, of course, he follows me.

Which is super unfortunate, since Ryder is waiting for me outside the door to my room and plainly visible from where we're standing.

For one moment – the time it takes my heart to beat – I consider ducking back into the elevator and making a quick escape. Maybe I'll move to another country, start over. Whatever I do, it's bound to be easier than the explosion that's about to go off.

"What's going on?" Ash comes to a dead stop, staring down the hall. Something tells me he's not admiring the artwork on the walls.

"Um…" *Oh, well done. What a great response.*

Ryder is staring just as hard as Ash, arms folded. If he juts his chin out any further, he'll injure his jaw. The image of a pair of stags preparing to lock horns flashes at the front of my mind's eye, and now I wish I had gotten back on the elevator, after all.

"Ryder came up to my room to grab something to eat," I explain, my words rushed, practically overlapping as they pour out of my mouth. "I ordered room service."

"Oh, really? And you wanted to be alone?"

"I don't like it when you act like I have to explain myself to you," I murmur. "And if this is ever going to work, I'm going to need it to stop. Got it?" He rolls his eyes but is smart enough to keep his mouth shut.

He is not, however, smart enough to get back on the elevator. No, instead he continues to follow me, at a bit of a slower pace this time. Like he's stalking his prey, and that prey is now Ryder instead of me. "Just grabbing a bite to eat, huh? In your room."

"That's why they call it room service."

"You got a problem with it?" Ryder demands. I wonder if he knows how much stronger his Boston accent becomes when he's angry or threatened.

"What if I do?" Ash counters. The tension in the air is practically enough to make my hair stand straight up. Somebody has to put a stop to this before it gets much worse.

"I have an idea." Probably the worst idea I've ever had, which is saying something considering the wreck I've made of my personal life. "Why don't you join us?"

"What?" they ask in unison.

"Sure. There's a ton of food coming, and maybe the two of you can talk things out, so there won't be any more uncomfortable confrontations in public."

And so I can prove I didn't ask Ryder to my room so we could get physical.

15

HARLOW

Spread out on the desk is a wild array of food. A cheeseburger and fries, fried chicken, meatloaf and mashed potatoes, spaghetti and garlic bread. There's also a grilled chicken Cobb salad – my order.

Once everything's laid out, Ash surveys the feast before looking at Ryder and raising an eyebrow. "Seriously?"

"I didn't know what I wanted. It all sounded good."

I take my salad and sit in the swivel chair behind the desk. It doesn't normally take me this long to open a plastic cup of blue cheese dressing, but then I'm not usually this intent on staying out of a potential argument. Which one of them will be the first one to start trouble? I'm betting on Ryder, but Ash still has a chip on his shoulder. It's obvious from the way he moves through the room — cautious, careful, guarded.

"Is there anything here you're more interested in than anything else?" he asks. I can appreciate his good manners, but it's all an act.

"Not really. Maybe the burger. A piece of chicken." Ash claims the pasta, then, and takes one of the two fried chicken breasts to eat on the side. He takes a seat on the bed, using the nightstand as a table. Ryder sits at the dresser, pulling up a small, striped armchair.

The atmosphere in the room doesn't exactly inspire an appetite. "So." I spear a few pieces of lettuce and avocado on my fork, glancing back-and-forth between them while I do. "What do you think of Seattle so far?"

"Is this really where Starbucks started?" Ryder asks.

"I think so." I look at Ash, but he only shrugs.

"I'd still rather go to Dunkin," Ryder decides before taking a huge bite of his burger.

"Big surprise," Ash mutters while twirling spaghetti on his fork and pretending he doesn't notice the glare I shoot him.

"Dunkin is an institution in the Northeast, isn't it?" I ask Ryder.

"Yeah, it is."

"I'd still rather have Starbucks," Ash decides, sounding sullen.

Well. Here's a conversation I would never have imagined. Arguing about coffee shops. I guess it's better than other things they could argue about.

"This is my first training camp." Neither of them react, too busy pretending to care about their food. "What can I expect?"

"It's hard work." Ash looks up. "Real hard."

"If you can't handle it," Ryder mutters.

"Stop," I whisper while shooting him a dirty look.

"He doesn't need to stop," Ash insists, sitting up and folding his arms as he gazes across the room that's not very big to begin with. The air is starting to feel awfully warm.

"I'm just saying." Ryder sets down what's left of his burger and wipes his hands, shrugging. "If you can't handle it, you can't handle it. That's the whole point. Pushing us as far as we can go."

"You always look at everything as a challenge, don't you?" I muse.

"Everything is a challenge."

"Main character energy if I ever saw it," Ash mutters, and it doesn't sound like a compliment.

"Wow. Great burn." Ryder begins to unfold his body, standing slowly without looking away from Ash.

"Don't do this." Honestly, I'm not even worried that they're going to get into a fight. I'm tired. I'm tired of having to get in the way. I'm tired of this macho bullshit. "I don't find any of this impressive, in case either of you were wondering."

"This isn't about you." Ash returns Ryder's combative stare as he stands. "This is about certain people running their mouth for years and finally getting an ass kicking."

"And you think you're the one who'll give it to me?" Ryder laughs as he takes a step closer to the bed, where Ash waits, arms folded.

"It would be my pleasure."

"Okay, this is stupid." And to think, I was really enjoying my salad. I have to leave it aside, jumping up to wedge myself between them before either starts throwing fists. "You're not going to solve anything this way. And I don't feel like getting blood on my nice bed." I was sort of hoping one of them might crack a grin, but they're both too busy being big, bad men to pay attention. What if they get in a

Pucking Disaster

fight? What if it gets out *why* they were fighting? No, I can't let that happen.

"I'm not kidding." With a grunt, I shove them apart, and at least now they're paying attention to me. "You're acting like teenagers. What you need to do is get past this. Move on."

Ryder scoffs. "It's not easy to get past it when I've got this asshole making shitty little comments all the time."

"Don't act like you don't do it," I remind Ash when he scoffs right back. "You love to start trouble."

He shrugs it off. "If you can't handle a little ball busting, I don't know what to tell you. I guess you forgot, that's what we've all done to each other since we started playing on the team together."

"This is different, and don't act like it's not. It's personal."

"Maybe you're a sore loser," Ash counters. "Did you ever think that could be the problem?"

"Nobody lost anything!" Except for me, maybe. I'm starting to think I've lost my mind. "For God's sake. Could somebody for once ask me what I want? I can tell you what I don't want, the two of you punching each other's lights out over me."

I don't know any other way to say it. I don't know any other way to get through to them. I only hope this isn't a mistake, because the last thing I want is to hurt either of them... again. "Do you want to know the truth? Do you want to hear what I think about things for once? Because until now, all I've seen is the two of you butting heads like two kids fighting over the same toy truck. You're treating me like a thing, like a possession. When really, I don't belong to either of you. But I do like you both. Though right now, I have to wonder why."

At least they're both quiet now, by some small miracle. Both staring at me, waiting to hear what I'll say next. "There's no reason for anybody to be jealous of anybody else when it comes to me, because I don't want to have to choose. I have no intention of choosing."

Ryder's mouth is open. Ash narrows his eyes. I honestly can't believe I just said that, but now that I have, I can't pretend it doesn't feel right. Sheer instinct is what's driving me now.

"What are you saying?" Ash tips his head to the side, almost scowling like he's trying to translate some ancient hieroglyphics.

"What does it sound like I'm saying?" When I look at Ryder, I find him just as confused. "I'm saying we could all sort of be together. That's what I want."

When neither of them reacts, instinct drives me again. This time, I reach for Ash's hand and place it on my chest, cupping my breast. Ryder growls — I don't even know if he realizes he does it – but before he can react further I take him by the back of the neck and pull him down for a long, deep kiss.

Is this completely insane? Probably. But dammit, it feels right. The energy flowing between us, binding us together. Ryder's tongue slides past mine while he buries a hand in my hair. After a second of hesitation Ash's hand moves, cupping my flesh, fondling me the way he always does so well.

I had no intention of things going in this direction. I really, truly didn't.

But here we are, and I'm finally starting to understand that there's no stopping this. There's no pretending it's not real. It is as real as the searing heat racing through me from head to toe, setting my soul on fire.

And it's a fire I have no intention of putting out.

16

RYDER

We're doing this, aren't we? We're actually doing this.

As much as part of me wants to end it, pull away and leave the room and pretend it never started, my feet are rooted to the floor. Maybe it's the way she tastes, the way she smells. Maybe it's the way I've been practically dying, waiting for the chance to kiss her again. She made it sound like this would never happen, like we were nothing but a mistake. But here we are now, with her tongue probing my mouth, and my hand buried in her hair.

Between the rush of sheer adrenaline coursing through me and my rapidly hardening dick, there's no chance of getting me out of here.

Especially with him here. I'm not letting him get her to himself. No way. He's not going to win.

Still, it's a little awkward when she breaks our kiss — her face is flushed, her eyes wide and full of a burning light — then she turns to Ash so she can kiss him the same way. What do I do now? It was a hell of a lot different when it was just me and two girls. I could enjoy watching them kiss and touch each other. I didn't get the sense that I was being forgotten or pushed aside.

All I can do is follow my instincts, and right now, they're telling me to put my hands all over her. Ash turns her in place and holds her still, the selfish bastard, wrapping his arms around her and clutching her against him.

There's nothing I can do but move behind her and press my dick into her ass, grinding against it. I lower my head and nuzzle her neck, and she reaches back to take hold of my neck. When she moves her hips, grinding against me, It's sort of like a victory. I'm doing something right here.

I have to touch her skin. I need to feel her. God, what is it about this woman? All of a sudden I'm half crazy, ready to throw her on the bed and conquer her. My hands are shaking with desire. I can barely hold back as I work them under her dress, bunching it up around her waist. Her deep moan pushes me on, makes me fondle her firm ass before working my fingers between her creamy thighs to where she's already wet, hungry.

She breaks their kiss, breathless. "Bed." I direct her to it and she lies down, then holds out her arms for both of us to join her. I take one side and Ash takes the other, both of us kicking off our shoes before exploring her with our hands, our mouths and tongues.

While it's weird doing this while he's here, as minute after minute passes with the three of us kissing and touching, I sort of get the point. I get to enjoy making her moan helplessly and run her fingers through my hair, but I also enjoy listening to her moans when Ash does something she likes. I would rather it be me she was moaning for, but there's something about the sound of her pleasure that gets me hard as a rock. There is nothing hotter than hearing a woman enjoy herself, and she is an expert at shutting out the rest of the world and focusing completely on what her body is feeling.

Like when I peel her skimpy panties away from her skin and slide them down her legs. She lifts her hips to help me before her thighs fall open for my fingers to delve through her slick folds. "Oh, yeah," she whispers while her head rolls from side to side. She's lost in another world. Ash looks up from her throat, where he was licking and nipping her skin, and in the split second our eyes meet, a silent challenge passes between us.

Her hips leave the bed when I ease two fingers into her tight channel, hooking them to massage her G-spot while using my thumb on her clit. "Oh, my God! Ryder!" After that, all she can do is moan helplessly, wordlessly, like she's speaking in tongues, while I work her pussy into a frenzy.

And as I do, I look at Ash again and lift an eyebrow. *Your move.*

A smirk passes over his lips before he pushes her dress up to her chest to reveal her perfect, heavy globes and the rosy pink nipples that tip them. He closes his lips around one of them, tugging a little, flicking his tongue over it before sucking hard. Meanwhile, his free hand runs over her thighs, her stomach, the curve of her ass.

"Come on," I growl in her ear as I work her, and my own breathing is coming faster already. "Come for me. Do you have one for me, baby? Let me hear it."

Ash turns her face away from me, his tongue darting out and licking her lips until she parts them, moaning loudly, jerking her hips harder to meet my strokes.

I know she's close when she starts tightening around my fingers. I lean down to whisper in her ear after running my tongue around the edge. "That's right. Come on my fingers. Get them nice and wet. Get them wet so I can taste you on them."

And that's when she howls, going stiff and clamping down around my fingers before the muscles begin to flutter. That's when she falls back against the bed, whimpering, her chest heaving, her body flushed.

At least I got the first orgasm.

Ash goes for the second, diving between her legs before I can and lapping up the juices that have dripped down her slit. With one hand, she holds his head close, but then she uses the other to rub my aching dick through my jeans. It's time to get rid of these, and I do it quickly, taking my shorts off with them before peeling my sweater off and tossing it onto the floor.

When she closes her tiny fist around my shaft, a wave of pure pleasure rolls over me and makes me move my hips, fucking her fist while we kiss slowly, passionately. My fingers graze her nipples, fingers dancing over the flat plane of her stomach until she writhes and moans into my mouth.

If I'm not careful, I'll lose it here and now. But it's not easy to stop what feels so good, so right. Even Ash's grunts add to the excitement, the heat. Watching him feast on her and hearing the effect it has… I never thought it could be like this. I can't tell myself I don't like it.

A few minutes ago, I was ready to kill him. Now we're in a competition to see who can make her come the hardest.

"Give it to me," she begs, opening her eyes just long enough to gaze into mine. "Give me your dick."

"Where do you want it?" Right now, I will do anything she wants. She holds my life in her hand.

She runs the tip of her tongue over her lips. "In my mouth. I want to suck it."

Fuck me. I hardly know this woman, this wanton, needy goddess. She's like a fantasy come true, begging for me, begging to pleasure me. And I give her what she wants – I'd be an idiot not to. I'm careful when I get on my knees, cradling her head in my hands and guiding myself between her parted lips.

She takes firm hold of me right away, running her tongue along the underside of my head and sucking greedily. "Ah, shit, yeah." My head falls back and I close my eyes to soak in the sensations she's stirring up. Between that and the sound of her pleasure, I'm in heaven right now.

She starts to lose her rhythm, sucking harder. I look down and watch her cheeks go hollow and her face go red. She's going to come again. I pull out at the last second so she can shout her release, shaking from the force, her hands twisting the blankets underneath her. It's maybe the hottest thing I've ever seen, watching her come, watching the way her body moves.

Ash reaches into his back pocket as he gets off the bed, pulling out his wallet before dropping his pants and shorts. He pulls a few condoms from his wallet and drops them on the bed.

"Who said you go first?" I grab for one of the foil packets and tear it open.

"Why don't we leave it up to her?" We both turn to Harlow, still spread eagle on the bed and looking like she got hit by a truck – but in a good way, in a messy hair, smudged make up way. She is gorgeous any other time, but now? Now she takes my breath away.

"I don't care who goes first," she whispers, sitting up before rolling onto her hands and knees and putting her ass on display. She parts her legs a little and gives us a clear view of her swollen, glistening lips, her quivering pussy. "I just need one of you inside me. Now."

I'm quicker than Ash and rock hard thanks to Harlow's expert sucking. I position myself behind her, kneeling on the bed and taking her hips in my hands. When he sighs, I offer him a brief shrug and a smirk before guiding myself inside her.

Oh, shit. I have to close my eyes as she envelops me in heat. "Oh, yeah, so good," I sigh, content to stay still for a second, to soak in the sensation. When she pushes back against me, I have to laugh – she knows what she wants, and she's in a hurry to get it.

Ash watches for a moment, stroking himself while I set my pace, taking her in long, almost lazy strokes. Making her feel every inch of me, invading her again and again until she moans my name. It's like music, hearing my name fall from her lips as I plunge in and out of her wetness. I'm a king. I'm a god.

"Put it in your mouth." I look up to find Ash in front of her, his back to the headboard, feeding her his dick. She takes it eagerly and he closes his eyes. I know that feeling because I experienced it only a few minutes ago. The way she uses her tongue is insane.

She sucks him just as eagerly as she did me, moaning, breathing fast, and soon there's nothing in the room but the wet, sloppy sounds of sex. My body slapping against hers, her mouth sucking Ash. All three of us, moaning, working together.

"I know you've got another one for me." I reach around, finding her clit and strumming it while I take her deeper, harder. Her cries rise in pitch until they're more like squeals smothered against Ash's dick, louder and louder until he pulls free and she turns her head to look back at me. "Fuck me…!" she begs, and I respond by digging my fingers into her hips and holding her still, pounding her with all my might until we're both lost and there's nothing I can do but let go while her greedy pussy milks me for all it's worth. I see stars by the time I'm finished, pulling out and pulling off the condom before almost collapsing next to her. She falls onto her side, tangled with me, and for a moment it's just the two of us. Ash may as well not be here. There's nobody in the world but us, and what we just shared.

Even when he takes his place behind her and pushes her closer to me with his first thrust, it feels right. To kiss her and caress her while he takes her from behind. "Does that feel good?" I whisper, brushing tangled hair away from her face, kissing her nose, her forehead, her mouth.

"Yes… Yes, so good…" she whines, closing her eyes, letting her head fall against my shoulder. We're both sweating a little. It makes our bodies slide easily against each other and her skin smell like a mixture of vanilla and musk. God, I could soak in her scent all night long and never get enough.

"Are you going to come for him? Can you come one more time?"

"I think so…"

"Good girl." My lips graze her jaw, her shoulder, her tits while Ash takes her harder with every thrust.

Her cries get louder, and her whimpers turn to moans again.

I'm not the man inside her, but that doesn't matter so much now. All I want is to encourage her, to watch her explode in pleasure again.

And she does, arching against Ash and straining almost like she's in pain before going limp against me. She's completely wiped out, totally lost. I've never seen anything so beautiful.

When Ash opens his eyes, coming to after his release, he looks straight at me. I don't know exactly what passes between us, but I do know one thing for sure, this isn't the last time we're going to do this.

And I can't say I mind.

17

HARLOW

I have to admit, the beginning of training camp isn't what I expected.

I've watched these guys work for weeks now. I've watched the drills the coaches have them run. I've watched scrimmage games — hours and hours and hours of scrimmage games. I thought I at least had a clue of what it would mean for the team to start training in earnest for the new season in a couple of months.

And I guess I did have a clue, but what I already knew barely scratches the surface of what I'm witnessing as I sit behind Coach Kozak, watching as he shouts orders to the team. "Hustle, hustle! Stretch those legs! What did I tell you lazy asses about calling it an early night?" He barks out a knowing laugh, while the players fly back and forth.

"One day you'll learn to listen to your coach, won't you? Shake off the cobwebs!"

And here I am, stifling a yawn. We didn't exactly call it a late night, the three of us, but I'm definitely feeling the after-effects this morning the way I always do after a long night of sex.

Ash flies past, and I have to fight back a grin. Luckily, the coach isn't paying attention to me as much as he is to the slowest of the guys. I notice Max is one of them and wonder how late he and Heather were up last night. I get the feeling he would rather take the coach's disapproval than his wife's disappointment. I can't say I blame him.

Coach settles back and lets the assistant coaches take over for a little while, picking up his insulated coffee cup and drinking deep. "What do you think of this place?" he asks, looking around the practice arena.

"Would I sound unprofessional if I said it's really cool?"

"I wouldn't have asked otherwise. It is cool."

I have to stifle another yawn. Late night or not, I'm not used to being up and out before seven in the morning. I don't even technically need to be here so early, but I want to make sure the guys know I'm part of the team. I'm one of them.

Alright, and maybe I'm a little paranoid.

If my hands are trembling, it's not because of the amount of caffeine I've consumed so far this morning. Just the thought of either Ryder or Ash doing or saying the wrong thing and spilling the beans makes my insides churn. I can trust them. I need to believe I can trust them.

But knowing those two, one of them will make some kind of a snide comment about their staying power, or something similarly stupid and snarky, and that will be the end of it. Because neither of them can stand down from a perceived threat.

They both have their own reasons why. I'm not sure of Ash's yet, aside from his cocky confidence and how fragile such confidence usually proves to be.

Ryder, I can easily diagnose. He has a lot to prove to himself after spending years fighting to prove his worth to others. He feels threatened, or challenged, and he erupts. Clearly, we need to do more work on those tendencies.

One of the assistants skates over and Coach Kozak deals with him, leaving me to brood on my own. We never really discussed anything last night. Neither of them confirmed that they want us to be a throuple or whatever it should be called. As much as I want to take the fact that we had sex as confirmation, I can't assume anything.

But let's say they did accept. That they want us to continue on the way we behaved last night.

When I remember how good it felt, how incredible, I can't be upset. If anything, my body hums with anticipation of being with them again. It's getting harder and harder to focus on my job around these guys.

I want to be with them. I do. And I would love it if I no longer felt the need to sneak around or lie.

But I can't shake the feeling that I'll end up with another full-time job. This time, it'll be a matter of juggling their egos. Making sure I don't give one of them more attention than the other. The idea takes me back to last night, when I had to get in between them to keep them from throwing fists. It was exhausting. Do I really want to invite that drama into my life?

And then there's Soren. The other piece of the puzzle. Does he know what happened? It would mean Ash going straight to him and reporting — I know they're close friends, but would Ash do that? Or Ryder could've told him this morning, in the locker room, but then Ryder understands how important it is to keep things discreet. I want to have faith in his good sense. I can't be in a relationship with anyone I don't trust.

Though that would mean calling this an actual relationship, and I'm not even sure I can or should do that.

We should talk over ground rules. Communicate. At least, that's what any decent therapist would recommend. I need to start putting this doctorate of mine to use.

I swear, it's like the universe is conspiring to throw curveballs my way. No sooner do I think of him, than Soren skates past and flashes a grin. I'm the only one sitting here, so it must have been directed at me.

There goes my paranoia again. That grin doesn't have to mean he knows about last night. It could just as easily be the result of what we've already done together in the past. He wants to make sure I know he's thinking about it. It doesn't have to be anything more than that.

Even if it feels like it does. But I'm feeling guilty and nervous. Everything's going to feel like a potential threat. Shouldn't I know better by now?

"He's looking good, isn't he?"

"What?" My head snaps around when Coach Kozak speaks to me. He is tracking Soren's progress with his gaze, not looking at me. Thankfully. My cheeks are so red and hot, I'm sure he would know something's up.

"Soren. He looks great out there."

"Yeah," I agree. "He's looking good."

"Think we could live without him for a while?"

It takes a second for what he's saying to sink in. That's what happens when you're busy worrying your secrets will be revealed. You miss what's right in front of you.

"Without him…?"

His head bobs up and down. "It's looking like the chances of him getting a two-way contract are pretty high. We might have to do without him for a while."

18

HARLOW

"Do you know that for sure?" I can't believe the way it feels like my whole life is hanging in the balance of what he says next. I shouldn't be this attached to any of the guys, but I can't help it. I care about Soren, too. I hate to think of him not being around.

It wouldn't be forever, though.

Unless it was. Unless the team decided to sign him permanently. Stranger things have happened.

If I care about him, I'll be happy for him. It's a good thing, an advancement, something he's worked hard for.

My stupid feelings have nothing to do with it.

"Not exactly sure, not a hundred percent," the coach tells me. I release the breath I am holding, though my worries aren't so easy to let go of. "But he's definitely a top contender."

"Who else are they looking at?"

"The team has expressed interest in a handful of players." He should be happy about this – I'm sure he is, in part. Mostly, though, he looks concerned. Like he's just as worried as I am.

He takes a seat in front of me and tilts his body so we can talk without him shouting. Of course, we want to keep this quiet until there's something more definite in the works. "Ash and Ryder are likely candidates, and they're looking at Danny and Michael, too."

Gazing across the arena, I notice the handful of strangers watching the players running drills. "Are they from the Orcas?" I ask out of the corner of my mouth, nodding slightly in their direction.

"Yeah, that would be them. They're paying attention."

What if all three of them are taken at the same time? I can't believe how much the idea hurts. I'm going to miss the hell out of them. Sure, they've been an almost constant source of worry and guilt ever since I first set eyes on them, but that doesn't mean I'm in a hurry to go through life without them, either. Only now do I understand how much I've come to look forward to running into them. Watching them play.

Wait. What am I thinking about? This is pitiful. It's also yet another reason why I had no business getting involved with them in the first place. I have a job to do, and instead of figuring out ways to cover the gap their absence will create, all I can do is think about my hormones.

"That's going to be a real challenge for us," I muse, trying to look into the future to see where this will take us.

"All the work we've done to balance their skills, and it might all be for nothing," he laments, rubbing his temples.

"It's not for nothing," Putting on a smile isn't easy, but he needs to see it. He needs encouragement right now, when he's so worried. He has his heart set on the team doing well this season. He's putting all of his effort into it. Not only because the owners want him to — and I'm sure they do, I'm sure there's got to be a ton of behind-the-scenes pressure I am unaware of.

He really wants this for them. Maybe for himself a little, but mostly for them. He believes in them. He wants to see them succeed. And now, there is the chance that a few of his players may get called up for a little while and stick a wrench in gears that have finally started moving smoothly.

"Of course, I haven't had time to start outlining new combinations yet, since you only first mentioned this yesterday on the plane. But with a little time, I'll find a way to balance the lines. We'll get through it – and they'll pull together, I'm sure."

"I want to believe that."

"Didn't you say it yourself yesterday, before takeoff? There's been a huge improvement in their attitudes. They're going to have to band together and cover the slack, so we'll frame it in the right context."

He arches an eyebrow. I'm glad to see it. If he's intrigued, he isn't worrying. "And what do you think that means? How would we get through to them?"

"They're a team. More than a group of individuals. They are one, cohesive unit. And they will be called upon to do what's best for the team. It might mean working a little harder. It might mean having to develop or strengthen skills in areas where they're lacking a little. But it's for the success of the team as a whole."

"You think it'll be that easy, eh?"

"I didn't say it would be easy," I admit, making him chuckle. "But I don't see why it has to be difficult, either. These guys work hard, and they work for each other. Not only for themselves."

I'm glad to see his expression smooth out a little. He is still stressed, but not as much as before. "You know, that's one thing I didn't count on," he finally says with a sigh.

"What do you mean?"

"When I hired you. I figured it was for the sake of the team. You would treat the players. You would make life easier for them."

He flashes a grin that warms my heart. "And here you are, talking me off the ledge."

"What can I say? This is what I do for a living."

"And you're damn good at it. I hate to think of heaping more work on your shoulders, though. We'll need to create contingency plans based on all possibilities, I'm afraid."

"You mean, if Soren's missing, we do this. If Ash is missing, we do that."

"Exactly. I shudder to think of both of them going at the same time. Just when we got the second line in order, too."

I nod, trying to focus on the team alone. I can't let my personal feelings leak into this. I've already done enough of that. "Hey, at least I have a little lead time. It's not like you're dumping this on me all at once, out of the blue."

Pucking Disaster

"Hustle out there!" His sudden shout makes me jump in surprise. He turns to me, apologetic. "Sorry. I swear, it's like my awareness is split at all times. Trying to keep an eye on them, trying to coordinate with the coaches."

"I can relate."

"You feel that way, too?"

"Sure." He has no idea how experienced I've become with splitting my attention.

"Yeah, I guess you do." He waves a hand, gesturing toward the players. "You want them to do what's best for them and fulfill their potential and all that, but there's also what's good for the team. Both of those things have to be managed at the same time. I guess that's a lot for you to handle all at once."

Sure. I'll let him believe that's all I meant.

"We'll figure it out. It will be alright." Am I lying to the man? Well, no — it's not a lie, because I have to figure it out. There's no other option.

Am I kidding myself, though? That could be what I'm doing. Telling myself what I need to believe. There's a very real possibility of biting off more than I can chew, but what's the alternative? Giving up? Not gonna happen.

"I hope you're right." Then he clears his throat, lowering his brow. "Of course, we'll keep this between us. I don't want them knowing yet."

"Of course. I'll make it a point to sit down over lunch and break the team down in terms of skills, strengths, weaknesses. It will be easier to shuffle everybody around that way." If anything, the more I talk about it, the stronger the electric buzz that's begun forming in the back of my head. A little tingle, nothing more, but it starts to spread the more I think about it.

An opportunity to prove myself. Sometimes, it's all a matter of reframing things. I can show the coach and everybody else what I'm made of by building these contingency plans.

Not to mention that it will be an excuse to take my mind off my personal issues. I'm here to work, anyway, not to get laid. Certainly not to complicate my life any further. Having the guys hundreds of miles away would uncomplicate things a little, come to think of it. But as I sit here and let that idea percolate while I observe training, all it does is make me sad. There's a longing that stirs in my chest when I imagine them being gone. I would miss them. Yes, I'd be happy for them. I would cheer them on. But I would miss them, too.

Maybe too much.

19

HARLOW

There is definitely something to be said for this weather.

What was chilly last night has turned pleasantly warm this afternoon. There's a breeze coming off the water beyond the restaurant's patio. It's absolutely delicious, and I smile to myself every time it stirs the fine hairs that didn't quite make it into my ponytail. What a stroke of good luck that it happens to be bright and sunny today, because I could use a little time out in the sun, soaking up some vitamin D while picking at a salad and racking my brain over the different holes we'll have to fill, depending on which players get a contract.

As I work, I can't help but think of a game on my phone. You move different blocks around to make space to allow a specific block to move out of the enclosure. It's all a matter of logic, looking ahead, imagining what each move will result in and how to work through that. Here I am, playing that game in real life, only with actual stakes.

But I like things like this. To be challenged, to stretch my limits. I guess that could be why I went for my doctorate in the first place. I could've gotten a perfectly good job with my masters, but I wanted more. I wanted to challenge myself.

Laughter draws my attention from the notes in front of me, and for a while, it's enough to watch a group of kids running around and playing tag, or something like it. A few people jog past on the path bordering the water, while others walk their dogs and chat happily.

I'm lucky, and it's times like this that drive the fact home. I get to sit here in the sunshine while I work. I get to solve problems on my time, wherever I want to work. How many people can say the same? When I look at it that way, it makes my petty problems seem insignificant.

"Hey there."

Speaking of petty problems. I shield my eyes with one hand, looking up at the sound of that voice. I already knew who it was – there's no mistaking the humor in it. It's like he's always in on a joke nobody else is aware of.

"Mind if I join you?" Soren gestures to the other side of the table I'm seated at.

"Be my guest." Right away I flip my notes over, but of course he catches me doing it.

"Working on a secret project?" He settles in wearing a smirk, dressed in jeans and a T-shirt, the picture of relaxation.

"You're all finished for the day?"

"You were in there. You saw how hard they were working us." He runs a hand through his damp, freshly-washed hair. "Yeah, we're all through for the day. Bright and early tomorrow, of course."

"How do you think it went?"

"Fine."

"That's good."

That's good? This is so stupid. It's like we've never met. Clearly, there is a lot hanging between us – and I'm afraid to open the can of worms. For all I know, it's a can of worms he's completely unaware of.

Though something tells me that gleam in his eye isn't the result of being glad his long day has come to an end.

"How are you liking Seattle?" He stretches his long legs out in front of him and crosses them at the ankles.

"It's great. I could sit out here all day."

"That is something I miss, living and working in Palm Springs. I don't get to spend nearly as much time outdoors as I would like. I mean, there's always the pool and everything, but I miss living in a more temperate climate."

"Did you do a lot of outdoor stuff back home?"

"Sure – but in my family, it was all about trips to Switzerland for skiing, that sort of thing."

"Like all the other rich, respectable people do?"

"Something like that." We share a smile, and it has the magic effect of loosening the tightness in my chest. Not all of it, but some of it.

He eyes my notepad. "So, really. What are you working on?"

"Something Coach wanted me to pay attention to, that's all."

"Trying to figure out how you'll replace me?"

"Wh-what makes you say that?" There goes the tightness again.

His brow wrinkles when he frowns. "It was a joke. Like, the team is going to fire me. Ha, ha."

"Sorry. I guess my sense of humor got lost on the way here."

"Did you not have enough room for it in your baggage?" I roll my eyes and he laughs, but that's fine. So long as I'm not the one who spills the beans about the two-way contracts. I don't know how much he or any of the other players are privy to. I don't want to cause trouble for myself or anybody else.

"It seems a shame," he muses, his tone light and playful. "Sitting here on this beautiful day, working."

"It's called having a job," I joke before looking up at the sky and wrinkling my nose. "It's starting to cloud up. Maybe I've gotten enough sun today, anyway."

"You know, all joking aside, Coach Kozak really depends on you. You've mellowed him out."

All I can do is arch an eyebrow. "Really? This is his version of mellow?"

"Believe me. This is him on Xanax compared to what we dealt with last season." He lifts a shoulder, his smile slipping as he looks over the water. "I understand it. He got a little more desperate with every game we lost. When you see your hopes slipping away a little bit at a time, what do you do? You close your fist tighter, hoping you can hold onto it."

"So he got louder, angrier, more frustrated."

"Exactly." His smile returns before he looks my way again. "But now you're here. Like Mary Poppins."

"Nobody ever mistook me for a Disney character."

"I don't know. I could see you carrying a carpet bag around. Reaching inside and pulling out exactly what everybody needs, when they need it."

Imagine that. A hot, gorgeous hockey player referencing Mary Poppins out of nowhere. The man has many layers. "And what could I pull out for you? What do you need?"

"Are you asking as a shrink, or as a friend?"

"Let's go with friend for now."

"As a friend?" He sighs, even grimaces a little, and I have a sneaking suspicion his answer isn't going to be completely sincere. He's got that devilish gleam in his eye again.

"This isn't a test. Just say whatever is on your mind," I urge.

"As a friend, I wouldn't mind a little honesty."

Did it get very warm out here all of a sudden? Or is it guilt coming through my pores in the form of sweat? "Honesty about what?"

"You know what."

"What if I don't?"

"Really? I thought we were better than that."

"Better than what? I'm serious." To think, all I was doing was sitting out here, minding my business. Eating my lunch, the rest of which is now forgotten. Trying to get a jumpstart on some work, so Coach Kozak doesn't have a stroke or worry himself to death.

Now, I have to decipher what Soren's trying to say. I don't want to jump the gun and say anything about what happened last night in case that's not what he's talking about. At the same time, it's sort of silly to sit here and pretend I don't know what he's getting at. I'm pretty sure I do.

"Really? After all we've been through?" He even has the nerve to pout like he's genuinely hurt. "I expected better of you."

"You're going to have to be more specific."

"What did you do last night?"

"I was in my room all night." That's the truth, too. I was definitely in my room. I wasn't alone, is all. That's the difference.

For a while, neither of us blinks. We stare each other down, silently daring the other to blink.

He cracks first, leaning in slightly, his brows drawn together and his eyes narrowing dangerously. It makes my mouth go dry and my heart race sickeningly. "You liar."

No. It's not supposed to be like this. He's not supposed to be angry. "Liar? Why would you —"

"Enough. Quit stalling, quit bullshitting me. Does it look like I was born yesterday? You really weren't going to tell me about what happened with Ryder and Ash?"

20

HARLOW

Oh, no. Can this get any worse? I'm absolutely sick to my stomach, sitting here while he glares at me with enough anger in his eyes to make me regret a whole bunch of things I can't change.

I've never been very good at disappointing people. I mean, I'm sure I have. I'm only human. But the idea of it makes me sick. When I was a kid, I just about worried myself into developing an ulcer when I had a particularly demanding English teacher. I wanted so much to please her, to be one of her favorite students. I wanted it so much that I lost sleep. I was too sick to eat some mornings, too concerned with making sure last night's homework was perfect.

Here I am all over again, worried that I disappointed somebody. Practically shrinking away from his angry, narrow-eyed stare.

His lips twitch first. His nostrils flare. Suddenly he's laughing, while I'm still lost.

"I'm just fucking with you," he insists, laughing harder when my mouth falls open. "Sorry. I couldn't resist."

"Are you serious?"

"I couldn't help it!"

"You're lucky we're in public, I swear."

"Really, I don't care about what happened last night." He's still chuckling by the time I calm myself down a little. "But I would like an invite in the future."

This is quite a surprising conversation. "Really? You mean that?"

"Only if you're interested, of course."

I feel like a balloon somebody popped, deflating against the chair. I swear, these men are taking years off my life. "How did you find out? They told you, didn't they?"

"No. They didn't. You did."

"No, I didn't."

"Sure, you did. Just now. I was suspicious, and you confirmed it for me."

"Son of a bitch!" I tip my head back and cover my face with my hands while he laughs — gently, at least, but still.

"You can be such a jerk when you want to."

"I won't argue with you there."

I should be mad at him. I should be absolutely furious, in fact. So why aren't I? Probably because he's so laid-back, with such a warm, easy-going sense of humor. He's the kind of person you can't be mad at for long. He's too charming.

And too hot. I'm not exactly proud of the fact that his hotness plays into things, but I can't help it.

"Can I ask why you were suspicious? What tipped you off?"

At first, he only smirks, telling me I'm going to have to work for any information I hope to gather, but I guess something about my expression or the way I asked convinces him to be honest rather than making me sweat it out. "To tell you the truth, they were so awkward around each other today."

"Really?" I can't help it. I am intrigued.

"Yeah, not the way it was last night, at the bar. More like they wouldn't make eye contact. They gave each other a wide berth, you know what I'm saying? There was no anger or resentment in the air. It was just… Mildly uncomfortable. And that's how I knew."

"You're a regular Sherlock Holmes."

"I know my friend. And I know Ryder well enough, too. We aren't as close as I am with Ash, but I've spent enough time with him to know when something's on his mind. The energy shifted."

"And you really don't mind?"

"Harlow, I couldn't care less who you sleep with. So long as they're good to you, and you're into it." He lifts a shoulder, pursing his lips. "And if I happen to be the man you choose to invite to your bed, lucky me."

I have a hard time believing it, but then he's never given me a reason not to trust him. I think it's more a matter of not being able to believe he's this casual about it. "I have to say, I wish I could be as laid-back as you are."

"It takes practice. And to be honest with you, I have spent most of my life being told I'm not serious enough. To be complimented on it is a refreshing change."

"Well, I'm glad I could do that for you."

"Come on. Let's get out of here." He jerks his chin, and I look in that direction to find the iconic Space

Needle towering over the skyline. "I've always wanted to check that out. How about you?"

"I was hoping to pay a visit while we were here, now that you mention it."

He eyes my work. "Can that wait a little while?"

"I don't see why not." Because really, it's so much more fun to hang around with him. I gather my things and toss out what's left of the salad, then we start off. The skies are getting darker all the time, so I would have to leave soon, anyway. When the first fat drops of rain start to fall, Soren leaves me standing under an awning in front of a pharmacy while he ducks inside to buy an umbrella.

I can't say I mind the excuse to huddle close to him as we walk, both of us sharing a single umbrella. With my arm tucked around his, it's almost sort of romantic. Walking in the rain, which falls gently and brings freshness to the air that mixes with his musky cologne.

"Would you rather get a taxi?" he asks.

"No, I like walking in the rain. So long as it doesn't turn into a downpour."

"I like walking in the rain, too. Something I've missed, living in the desert."

"That's true. I can't remember the last time I had to use an umbrella."

"I know you don't mind getting wet." When I scowl up at him once we've stopped at a red light, he has the decency to grimace. "Sorry. Bad joke."

"Yeah, a little bit." But aside from shaking my head and scowling, there's not much I can do. Something tells me if I'm going to be spending time with him, I need to get used to his sense of humor.

The closer we get to the Space Needle, the thicker the crowds. Lots of people want to take pictures at the base, cameras pointing upward. I crane my neck to look up as far as I can, but I get a little dizzy and end up holding onto Soren for balance.

"You sure you want to do this?" he asks with a warm chuckle.

"Sure. No sweat. I'm not afraid of heights."

"Maybe I am."

"Don't worry. You have me to keep you safe." Something in his gaze when he looks at me leaves me wondering if I'll be safe. There's that familiarity, that faint hunger. The sense that half of what goes on between us is double entendre, flirting, leading to something else. It shouldn't, right? At least, not until I've had a conversation with the other two men in my life and figure out what the hell is going on.

He's generous enough to buy tickets for both of us, and once that's done, we get on the elevator to take us to the top. "I've heard there's an event where you can climb all the stairs, instead of taking the elevator," he tells me as we rise through the air.

"You've done your research, huh?"

"I like to be prepared when I visit a new place." And even that is charming. The way he always wants to be prepared.

The elevator doors open and we step out, and everything I was thinking or wondering or wanting is swept away. "Wow." It's all I can say once the breathtaking view captivates me, stealing the breath from my lungs.

"It's incredible, isn't it?" For once, it doesn't sound like he's kidding around. Like there's finally something worth being serious about.

"It's gorgeous." Even against a slate-gray sky, there's something magical about being this high up, overlooking everything around us.

"Imagine all the people down there," he murmurs, sticking close by my side as we walk slowly around the circular deck to get a full view. "Living their different lives. Everyone pretty much wants the same thing, don't they? We want to be loved, we want to be appreciated. We want to love in return – everyone needs something to love, even if it's a pet or a favorite plant."

"Something to take care of," I offer.

"Exactly. There are things we need — shelter, food, water. A sense of purpose."

We come to a stop, and his sigh is heavy. "Why do we have to complicate things? We are all the same. We all need and want the same things. Why do we have to make it difficult?"

I could go into a long speech about psychological needs, about the ego and how it makes us believe we're separate from everybody else. How the human mind evolved over thousands and thousands of years.

Something tells me my expertise isn't needed right now.

He's a much deeper thinker than I imagined. Combined with everything else I already know about him, I can't help wanting to learn more. The attraction goes far beyond the physical.

"What do you think?" he asks when we come to a stop. "Was it worth the trip?"

"I think so."

"Good. If you're going to forget about your work for a little while, you might as well have a good time while you're doing it."

I know it's happening before it happens. When the energy shifts, when suddenly Soren's face fills my world. When he leans down, when he places a hand against the small of my back and holds me firmly in place. When the tiniest little smile touches the corners of his mouth before it meets mine.

I can't pretend to be insulted or shocked that he's kissing me.

I can't pretend not to kiss him back, either.

21

HARLOW

There's something painfully sweet about all of this. It's so natural, being with him, giving in to the unmistakable chemistry we share. It was always going to be like this, wasn't it? Our time together was always going to end in a kiss. A deep, slow kiss, as relaxed and unhurried as the man kissing me. I don't even normally go for these sort of public displays, but I can't bring myself to stop it. At least, not until I feel him growing against my hip.

That's what makes me stop, even as my heart sinks when I do. That's what makes me look him in the eye – he's grinning, of course, having gotten what he wanted. My lips throb along with the rest of me. Including parts that would like a lot more attention – the sooner, the better.

But that would be immature. Childish. Maybe even selfish, when I think about it, since I still don't know exactly what Ash and Ryder want. Hell, I'm not even sure exactly what I want, which should probably be more important.

I will not sleep with this man. At least, not now. I can't create another complication for myself. I need to be smart, if only for my own sake.

I have to take a step back to clear my head, so I turn away to look out over the city spread out under me. My heart is racing, my head spinning. It has nothing to do with a fear of heights, either.

"Are you alright?" There's genuine concern in his voice as he strokes my hair – gently, carefully. I have to fight the urge to lean into his touch.

"Sure. Just catching my breath."

"I didn't come on too strong?"

I only laugh softly, touching a hand to his chest. "I'll let you know if you're coming on too strong. Sound good?"

"Sounds good." But there's a light in his eyes that tells me he's not satisfied. He's not going to leave it there. I don't think I want him to, either – but I've only ever gotten in trouble by blindly following what my body tells me, right? I only end up regretting it later. I don't want that this time. I want to wake up in the morning and be able to look at my reflection without wincing.

He must see the conflict I'm facing, because he smiles a little before letting out a sigh. "Let's get out of here. What do you say?"

"What did you have in mind?" I can't help but be suspicious.

"I was thinking of getting a drink. We're off for the rest of the day, right?"

He might be, but I'm not. Right now, though, the idea of sitting down and scrambling my brain while trying to come up with a solution to our problems doesn't exactly appeal to me. I'll only end up wishing I had taken him up on his offer.

"Okay. But I'll buy my own drinks."

"Far be it from me to stop you."

"It's only fair," I reason as we head back to the elevator. "You bought my ticket to get up here."

"How refreshing. A woman who doesn't expect me to pay for everything." He's back to being his playful, carefree self. I couldn't be more grateful. The last thing I want is to deal with a bunch of questions and demands.

Instead, we stop in at a bar a couple of blocks from the Space Needle. It just happens to be the first place we stumble upon, and we settle in at a corner table with our drinks to talk more about anything and everything that comes to mind. Sports, yes, but also life itself. Movies, music. He lights up parts of my brain no other man ever has, now that I think about it.

"I still haven't shown you my wine collection," he reminds me while sipping on a Chardonnay that pairs perfectly with the cheese platter he ordered. I'm glad I followed his recommendation and ordered a glass for myself.

"By all means. I would love to see it."

He leans in, wearing a playful grin. "There are a lot of things I'd like to show you at my place."

"Oh, really?" I pull back, narrowing my eyes. "Like what? Your bed, maybe? Is that what you had in mind?"

"Doctor! I'm shocked at you. Putting those ideas in my head." He clicks his tongue and shakes his head until there's nothing I can do but laugh before he catches my mouth again with his very warm, very sweet lips.

Is it possible for a heart to sink and soar at the same time? Because I'm pretty sure that's what mine does. I wish he wouldn't make it so hard to resist him, but at the same time, I can't pretend I don't like the feeling of his lips against mine. It's almost comforting, how natural and good it feels. The way he lights up my body and my mind. It's a potent combination, and I am afraid I am helpless against it.

A second glass of wine loosens me up even more, and by the time the bar starts filling up, I know it's time to go. I'm practically giddy from the wine and from his nearness. It's getting harder to remember why I told myself we shouldn't happen.

"Maybe we should go back to the hotel," I suggest as casually as I can – but not casually enough, apparently, since his eyes light up right away. "Because I'm tired," I tell him in a firm voice. "It was an early morning."

"And you didn't get much rest last night, did you?" He holds up both hands, laughing gently while I scowl. "Sorry. Couldn't resist."

"Maybe try a little harder next time." He puts on a solemn face that only makes me laugh, because it looks so out of place on him. He's impossible to stay mad at. I might be in more trouble than I ever anticipated with this guy.

The rain has turned into a fine mist. I don't mind the excuse to huddle close to him as we walk, that much is for sure. He puts his arm around my shoulders and holds me closer, leaving me torn between loving the nearness and hoping nobody catches us out here on the street. Seattle is a big city with lots of people

Pucking Disaster

in it, and I'm sure the odds of anybody running into us out here are slim… but my luck hasn't exactly been terrific, either, has it?

My sudden concern translates to a stiffening of my body, which Soren picks up on right away. "What's on your mind?" There's nothing demanding in the question. It's gentle, the sort of thing one friend would ask another.

"Just wondering what the coach would think if he saw us like this."

"He would think I'm being a gentleman and escorting you back to the hotel under my umbrella." When he says it like that, I can almost believe him.

Just like I can almost believe Soren's invitation to his room is totally innocent. "What do you say? Just to hang out," he insists as we come to a stop in front of the elevator and he presses the button to take us up.

"Why do I not believe that?"

"You must be a very suspicious person." I narrow my eyes and he chuckles, shrugging good-naturedly. "I just don't want to say goodbye, that's all. I like having you to myself for a little while. Maybe I'm greedy, but I can't help it."

I wish he hadn't asked, and I wish I didn't want so much to take him up on it. Rather than answer right away, I stall for time by going through my bag, looking for my phone. It's buzzed a few times this afternoon, but I ignored it in favor of giving him my full attention.

And now I see what I missed, and it makes me grit my teeth. Five missed calls, half a dozen text messages. All of them from either Ryder or Ash.

Ryder: I want to see you.

Ash: Let me know when you're back in your room. I want to talk.

Ryder: Where are you? Is everything OK?

Ash: I stopped by your room and there was no answer when I knocked. Are you alright?

I cannot deal with this right now. I don't like the feeling of being ambushed, for one thing, and I'm not a fan of being put on the spot. That's how this feels. Like they're demanding something from me on their time, when they want it.

"Well?" We step onto the elevator, and Soren's finger hovers over the button for his floor. "Are you coming with me, or are you making a mistake and going back to your room alone?"

"Who said it would be a mistake? You've got a mighty high opinion of yourself."

"Guilty." He holds up his hands in mock surrender. "I never said I didn't."

Right now, the idea of hanging out with him is a lot nicer than answering a bunch of questions that I'm sure will sound more like demands. Rather than give him an answer, I press the button for his floor. He smiles and says nothing. I'm sure he feels like he's won. Why bother ruining it with a quip?

As the elevator rises, taking us closer to what I need to believe won't be a mistake, his hand finds mine and closes around it.

And I'll be damned if my body doesn't respond in the strongest way, my racing heart and moistening pussy reminding me why it's no use trying to fight the inevitable. This is how it was always going to turn out.

And it's not like this would be my first mistake, anyway. I'm starting to get used to making them.

22

SOREN

I've never had to work so hard to get into a woman's panties.

And it's never felt so rewarding to finally break down her walls. The greatest victories are the ones that don't come easy, right? That must be why I'm on top of the world by the time we're inside my room with the door closed and my hands on her, just like I've wanted them to be all day. A few little kisses in public aren't nearly enough to quench my thirst for her. She has no idea what she's done to me and what she continues to do every time I'm with her.

"Maybe we shouldn't do this." Even as she's saying it, though, she's dropping her bag on the floor and pulling off her oversized cardigan, tossing it over the chair in front of the desk.

"We can stop whenever you want." Meanwhile, I work my hands under her t-shirt, my already racing pulse picking up speed when I touch bare skin. I lift it over her head, and she raises her arms to help me, then links those arms around my neck and pulls me down for another kiss while I unbutton my jeans, kicking off my trainers while I do. This can't happen quickly enough. I've been yearning for her for days, dreaming about her, jerking off in the shower with the memories of her body to console me through my loneliness. I never felt lonely before I met her. I never had a reason to. I never met anyone worth missing this much, wanting this much. So much that I'm willing to throw aside everything else for her sake.

I take one of her hands and use it to cup my dick through my shorts. We both groan when our kiss deepens, tongues tangling, teeth clashing. Like we're fighting for control neither of us wants to give up.

There's a wicked gleam in her eye when she breaks the kiss and lowers herself to her knees, reaching behind her to unhook her bra so I can ogle her tits before she takes the waistband of my shorts and pulls them down. Slowly, so slowly. It's torture. I have to grit my teeth against the impulse to hurry her – some things are worth savoring, anyway. I don't want to rush through this.

There is nothing like the rush of indescribable relief when I spring free, swaying in front of her face. Our eyes meet, and I want to turn away from the intimacy of it, the feeling that this woman owns me somehow. She knows me, she understands me, and I would do anything for her. Anything at all, no matter what she asks. It's powerful enough to make me sway on my feet, that feeling, but it fades to the background once she takes me into her mouth and pushes everything else away.

"Harlow… You're so good to me…" She moans in response, and the vibrations from her mouth race through me. Her head bobs up and down in a steady rhythm while her tongue massages my underside, swirling in circles over the bundle of nerves beneath my head. It's pure bliss that I wish would last forever.

I grit my teeth, holding on to make it last. "So good… So good, Harlow…" Soon it's too good, though, and as much as I want her to keep going I pull out and raise her to her feet, kissing her deeply in appreciation. She melts against me, tits against my chest, her hip rubbing my straining dick until my knees go weak.

At first, the idea of putting her on the desk and fucking her until it breaks almost wins. I even place my hands on her hips, ready to lift her.

But it's the sight of the sliding doors on the other side of the room that catch my imagination and won't let go. She barely has time to gasp when I wrap my arms around her slim body and lift her off her feet, carrying her the short distance.

"What are you doing?" she whispers, red faced when I put her down in front of the glass.

"Don't worry. Nobody can see. The light's off." She's still sputtering her protests while I lower her leggings and the thong underneath them. But she doesn't stop me, because deep down inside, it turns her on, the idea of us doing it in front of the world.

The hotel is shaped like a U, with my room facing rooms on the other side of the wide courtyard. Those windows face mine, and to the right, the Seattle skyline is topped by dark clouds.

I turn her toward the glass and step up behind her, running my hands down her sides, my dick sliding between her ass cheeks. "Come on, good girl," I whisper in her ear, one hand snaking around to cup her hot, wet pussy. "Don't tell me you've never imagined something like this. I know how bad you can be."

She's lost in sensation, whimpering in approval as I rub her mound with one hand and cup her tits with the other, playing with the nipples, kissing her neck until she spreads her legs wide and braces herself against the glass with both hands.

"That's right," I grunt, dragging my head through her wetness before probing her entrance. "Open yourself up to me. Show me how bad you can be."

She gasps when I invade her, then leans against the glass with a deep, throaty groan. I would swear she's tightening around me already, drawing me deeper. There's nowhere in this world I'd rather be than buried balls deep in her, listening to her moans as she loses control one deep thrust at a time. As she gives herself to me, letting me do things to her, and with her, she would never have imagined.

Like now, splayed out for the world to see, her tits pressed against the glass while I take her hard, holding her in place with my body, pumping my hips frantically. I take her jaw in my hand and pull her head back, tilting it until our mouths align. Soon her groans are lost in my mouth, blending with my own until she pulls back and comes with a shuddering cry, almost sobbing as she leans against the glass while I continue pumping deep into her rippling heat.

I don't know what does it. A sudden flicker of light across the courtyard? It draws my eye, and even in my lust-fueled haze, I can't mistake the person now watching from their window. A person who looks a hell of a lot like my best friend. He's standing there, watching, his mouth hanging open.

Is it wrong that I want to laugh? Even when he goes for his phone, it's almost enough to take me out of the moment. But it doesn't. Not when she's gripping me so tight, trying to milk my dick, pushing back against me.

Another light flickers two floors down from Ash's room. A man stands at the window with a phone held to his ear. A man who happens to be Ryder. Now they're both watching – and considering Harlow is still coming down from her high, I don't think she's noticed.

And I'm not about to stop. No, I want them to know she's here with me. I want them to know she's mine right now. I mean, what are they going to do about it?

23

HARLOW

This is so wrong, but it feels so good.

Maybe that's why it feels as good as it does, because I know it's depraved. Spread eagle against the glass, knowing there's a chance of being seen but doing it anyway. I'm lost in a haze of sensation, already building to a second orgasm that feels like it will be stronger than the one I'm still trembling from.

"So tight," Soren whispers in my ear. "Fuck, you feel so good." I let my head fall back against his muscular shoulder while he continues moving inside me, pushing me a little closer to the edge with every strong thrust.

"Fuck me," I beg, spreading my legs a little wider to brace myself as he pummels me with relentless thrusts. Something inside me loves being taken like this, used by a hot jock with abs of steel and a dick that fills me so well. Maybe because I know he would never hurt me, really. There's still the thrill of thinking he might, he could. Just like somebody could see us.

Somebody sees us.

All it takes is opening my eyes and looking across the courtyard. Someone has their light on, and they're watching, standing smack dab in the middle of the sliding glass door and staring up at us.

"Soren!" I gasp, reaching behind me to swat at him with both hands. "Wait! Somebody's watching!"

No. Not just somebody.

It's incredible how quickly all thoughts of pleasure can dissolve and be replaced with cold, brutal horror. "Ash! Soren, he's watching!"

"Let him watch." He's still moving, thrusting harder, faster.

"Wait, It's not just him!" Because there's another light on — oh, no, this couldn't possibly get worse, but here it is, right in front of my face. "It's Ryder! Oh, my God!"

This time when I shove him away, he pulls out, stumbling backward while I frantically reach for my cardigan and punch my fists through the sleeves. It barely covers my butt, but it's better than nothing.

"Oh, my God, this is terrible! How many other people were watching?"

"Don't worry." He sits next to me on the bed and puts a hand on my knee. "Nobody else was watching. Just them. It's okay."

"You sound awfully sure of yourself."

And then it hits me. Man, there is something to be said for all the blood leaving your brain and traveling south when you're aroused. Otherwise, there's no way it would've taken me this long to figure out what's really going on.

I jump up from the bed, shaking and point a trembling finger at him. "You knew! You knew they were watching!"

"Harlow —"

"Tell me the truth! You knew, didn't you? Or else how could you be so sure no one else was watching? You don't seem surprised at all. Tell me the truth, dammit."

His head falls back and he stares at the ceiling, blowing out a heavy sigh. "Okay, so I knew they were there."

"I'm going to be sick."

"It's not like that. Harlow, come on."

I ignore him, stumbling to the bathroom and going straight to the sink to splash cold water on my face in hopes of staving off the wave of nausea that's gripping me. There's nothing like the sting of cold, hard reality to shake a girl out of her hormone fueled insanity.

"Harlow, come on." The son of a bitch is even laughing as he saunters through the open door, still naked and even semi-hard. "You're blowing this all out of proportion."

"How can you say that? You knew they were watching and you didn't say anything? What is wrong with you?"

"It was funny."

"Was it?" I turn toward him, folding my arms. "Explain to me what was so funny about it. Be specific. Where was the humor in this?"

"Come on," he groans. "You don't have to make such a big deal about this."

"Answer me!" I bark loudly enough for his eyes to go wide. "Explain the joke to me. Why is it funny that they were watching and you knew and you didn't tell me?"

"It wasn't even all that long."

There goes the nausea again, sweeping over me. "How long?"

"Really, no time at all."

"How long?"

"Was I carrying a stopwatch?" He throws his hands into the air before raking his fingers through his hair. "It was funny. I figured they'd be jealous. It's not like neither of them have ever seen you naked before."

"Unbelievable. You are absolutely unbelievable! What if they weren't the only ones?"

"You knew damn well it was possible, but that didn't stop you. And it shouldn't have. Who cares?"

"I care! Why doesn't that matter?"

"You didn't care before," he retorts with a smirk. I could kill him for it. "It was a thrill, wasn't it? There's nothing wrong with that. You can't keep doing this, you know."

"Doing what?"

"You're all about it in the moment, and then you get cold feet and do an about face afterward. That's not fair, either. Don't you get it?"

"You are not going to turn this around on me. I deserved to know when you knew. But no," I rant, throwing my hands into the air like he did. "No, you would rather make a joke about it. Like this is all some great, big pissing contest. You wanted to make sure they knew I was with you and not with them.

And you know what? That's fine. So long as I'm aware. And I wasn't. You took my choice away, and I can't accept that. Do you understand what I'm saying?"

"I understand you are making a much bigger deal out of this than it needs to be."

"You don't get to decide that." And now, I can't understand what I ever thought was so attractive about this devil-may-care attitude of his. Not everything is a joke, but he doesn't seem to understand that. Or he doesn't want to.

I want to get out of this room, but I'm too ashamed to show my face outside of it. For all I know, they could be on their way here right now, and I shudder to think how that confrontation would turn out. "Why do I keep doing this?" I whisper to myself, staring at my reflection.

"This doesn't have to be the end of the world," he reminds me from over my shoulder.

"Was I speaking to you?" I snap. "No. I don't think I was. I'm not sure I want to speak to you ever again."

I expect him to argue some more when his mouth opens.

To my surprise, his shoulders fall and a look of sadness washes over his face. "It matters that much to you?"

"Yes. Have I been talking to myself? I'm humiliated. You should have told me when you knew they were watching. At least I could have decided for myself if I wanted to keep going or not. Do you see what I'm trying to say?"

"Fuck." He looks at the floor, running his hand over the back of his neck. "I didn't think of it that way. I didn't think at all."

"No, you clearly didn't." I wrap my arms around myself, trembling. "And what if there were other people watching?"

"I swear, I didn't see anyone else. Seriously. Just the two of them. Ash saw us first, and then he called Ryder."

"Oh, my God." I have a headache. I'm still nauseous. When compared to the mistakes I've made one after the other ever since landing this job, this one tops them all. I couldn't have predicted what would happen, but I could've guessed. I am not a stupid person. Why do I keep doing stupid things? "I'm so embarrassed."

"I still don't think you have anything to be embarrassed about." I shoot him a filthy look, and he winces. "But I am sorry. Truly. I didn't mean to hurt you."

"No, I know you didn't." After all, he didn't even give it a thought. In the moment, all he cared about was one-upping his friends. Letting them know it was his turn. Like I'm some floozy for them to pass around.

And if that's what he thinks, it's nobody's fault but my own. I've let them treat me that way, after all.

"Now what am I going to do?" I whisper. All hopes of being taken seriously by the team are vanishing like smoke in the wind.

"Honestly?" He follows me out of the bathroom and stands beside the bed when I sit and put my head in my hands. "They have no business giving you shit about it. You can do what you want. And again, it's not like neither of them have ever seen you like that."

"I know." I lower my hands with a sigh. "I guess if anybody was going to see us, they are the best option. That still doesn't mean I'm okay with it. I should've had a choice whether I wanted to keep going. I'm so mad at you for that."

"And I promise, I won't ever do that to you again. It was unfair and childish." Wow. I can't believe he's actually so serious about it. Did I get through to him? Will wonders never cease?

"And so what if they're a little jealous?" he points out, and it's no surprise that he can't keep from smirking. "Let them be. They don't own you. We were just having fun."

"That's true. Oh, God, they're never going to let me live this down."

"Sure, they will." There's his relaxed, carefree attitude shining through. "They'll get over it."

A sudden, loud banging on the door makes me think otherwise. "Great." He pulls on his shorts before going to the door, while I close my sweater a little tighter.

The way his posture changes as he looks through the peephole tells me what I need to know before he says a word. He turns away from the door, shaking his head. "It's both of them. And they look pretty pissed."

Terrific. This is just what I needed.

24

HARLOW

"Don't let them in," I whisper fiercely. My heart's hammering and my hands are shaking while my head swings back-and-forth in a frantic search for... what? The open closet door reveals a complimentary bathrobe which I put on after tossing my sweater onto the bed. This covers more of me. It's just a standard terry cloth bathrobe, but right now, it feels like armor. And I need every scrap of confidence I can pull together if I'm going to face a couple of angry jocks who right now are practically banging the door down.

"Would you give it a second?" Soren calls out — then, because he's a real jerk when he feels like it, he throws me a wink before adding, "She hasn't finished coming yet!"

Oh, I want to die. "Could you not?" I whisper, cinching the belt on the robe and running my hands through my hair in hopes of pulling myself together enough to face them. This is beyond humiliating. I mean, it's one thing for them to have witnessed what we were doing, but that doesn't mean I need to be all flushed and messy. It would be like spiking the ball after reaching the end zone.

"We just want to talk!" Ash calls out. Good lord, is anybody else walking down the hall and seeing this? What if Coach Kozak runs into them out there? What if, what if, the questions are enough to drive me out of my skull.

"You better let them in, or we're going to have security up here in a minute." And as generally miserable as the situation is, it could be much, much worse. How would we explain this to the coach? Security coming up here because somebody complained about the noise in the hall, only to find me in a bathrobe and Soren in his underwear while another two players fought and shouted about it. This is the sort of situation that's ripe for gossip, too. Who knows how much uglier the story could get by the time it works its way through the entire team? Like a huge, messy game of Telephone.

I'm standing with my arms folded over my chest by the time Soren unlocks the door and opens it to reveal a glaring pair of men on the other side. Ash wastes no time barreling into the room, pushing past Soren in a hurry to face off with me. Ryder, I notice, takes his time. For once, he's the one being more thoughtful.

"What the hell is this all about?" With his hands on his hips, Ash glares at me. "What was that little scene about? Are you trying to show off for the whole hotel now? Are we not enough?"

"Come on, man." Ryder is more subdued, leaning against the desk with his hands shoved deep in his pockets. Somehow, his reaction stings worse than Ash's – I mean, the man is glaring at me like I'm some lost soul, a fallen woman or something like that, but that's easier to dismiss than Ryder's quiet disappointment.

"You really need to get a little perspective," Soren tells him. No big surprise, he's laughing. "Why is everything so urgent and extreme? Maybe you should talk to a therapist."

"You need to stop," Ash warns him, raking fingers through his dark hair before pointing a finger at his friend. "Not everything is a big joke, you know. Some of us actually give a shit."

"Who says I don't give a shit?" Soren spreads his arms in a shrug before plopping onto the bed, wearing a shit eating grin that makes me grind my teeth a little. "I do. I care a lot. But I also know when a situation calls for excitement, and when it doesn't."

He turns to me, lifting an eyebrow. "Wouldn't you agree? It can't possibly be healthy to fly into a fit over every little thing." There's glee twinkling in his eyes.

"You're not wrong," I venture, shifting my attention to Ash. "And on a personal note, I don't like having people yell in my face. I'm not a child."

"Do you actually give a shit or not?" Ryder's voice is quiet, almost flat, but there's another truth in his gray eyes. They're troubled. Seeing him like this makes my heart ache. Damn that Soren. I don't think I did anything wrong by having sex with him — I mean, no, I shouldn't be sleeping with the team members, but that's another story. I made no promises to anybody, and they have made no promises to me. In that respect, I am blameless in this.

But he had to go and rub it in.

"Of course, I care." I murmur as I clutch the robe a little tighter, close to my throat. "I care very much."

"You did a really good impression of it just now, up against the glass." Ash's face goes redder with every word. "What was that supposed to be? A show?"

"Okay, that was all me." Soren holds up his hands, chuckling when Ash glares at him. "She didn't know you were watching. But I did."

"What the fuck is wrong with you?" Ash demands. Even Ryder looks pissed, standing up straight and pulling his hands from his pockets to show off the fists now hanging at his sides. It's like somebody flipped a switch and there's now an electric charge running through the room.

Just about every red flag in existence starts waving in my head, and I make it a point to get between them quickly. "Okay, okay, it was a bad joke – and I'm still angry with you about it," I add, shooting him a dirty look. "It was uncalled for, and it was cruel, and I don't appreciate being used in your little jokes."

"I wasn't exactly thinking clearly. There was no blood left in my brain. It had all traveled south." He offers a playful shrug that doesn't do much to help the situation.

"Forget all that." Ryder waves off the joke, shaking his head at me. "You didn't answer my question. Do you care at all? Or are you just using us for a good time?"

I don't know if it's the question or the accusation behind it that makes me cringe. "It really hurts that you would ask me that. Don't you know better by now?"

"Honestly, no. I don't. Because you keep saying one thing, then doing another. I don't think I'm out of line, wondering if this is all one big joke."

"I would like to hear the answer to this, myself." Ash dips his chin, challenging me with an angry look from beneath lowered brows. "What are you getting out of all of this? The back-and-forth, the changing your mind all the time. What is the point?"

I don't like this. Being interrogated, glared at like I committed a crime. At the same time, if I were in their shoes, I'd probably do the same thing. I would want to know why.

"Well?" Clearly, I'm not allowed to give any thought, since Ash is demanding answers. "What are your intentions here?"

"Honestly… I don't know." Sure, it sounds lame, but it's the truth. I offer a helpless shrug, looking at each of them in turn. "I don't know what my intentions are, because I haven't thought that far ahead. All this time, I've been sort of going with the flow. You know? Seeing where this goes. You're looking for a plan? You're looking in the wrong place. How can I plan when all I've done all this time is tell myself how wrong this is?"

"That hasn't stopped you," Ash snorts.

"No, it hasn't," I retort. The man is determined to drive me crazy. "As you well know. Why am I the enemy right now? That's what I need to know. I don't want to hurt anybody. I'm sorry. Like I told you, I didn't know you were watching. It was all his idea."

"That's not an answer. Stop dancing around the question, would you?"

"I'm telling you, I don't know." I have to turn away, since I can't stand being glared at like this. Somehow, the world beyond the glass door keeps moving, with everybody out there living their normal lives with no clue of the drama that's going on up here. Lucky them. "Why isn't it enough that I like all of you? I like you so much, I'm willing to take a huge chance. Doesn't that matter?"

"Yeah, but you keep taking those chances," Ryder points out, "and you keep acting like this is it, like if you want to keep your job, we have to keep it quiet. But then you go and do something like that, up against the glass where anybody could see you. So yeah, it sort of makes me scratch my head and wonder where you're really coming from."

He is so right. Do I have some subconscious desire to sabotage myself? Is that what this is all about? Because right now, it's the only thing that makes any sense. No matter how many times I've told myself this is wrong, it hasn't stopped me from giving in during a weak moment — many weak moments.

"You're right," I admit, still staring out at the rainy afternoon. "I keep going back on my word to myself, and that needs to stop."

My heart is heavy as I turn around to look at the three of them. Soren is still sitting on the bed, watching me intently. Ash stands in the center of the room, arms folded, feet at shoulder-width. He is still jonesing for a fight. Here I was, thinking Ryder was supposed to be the confrontational one.

He stands silent at the foot of the bed, and I wish I could get a read on what he's thinking. He's been so quiet, almost ominous. Somehow, that worries me more than an outburst would, because at least an outburst would seem within his character.

"This has to be the end," I decide. "I mean it now. I like all of you, and I like being with you, but all it's doing is causing problems like this — and I know I sound like a broken record, but this really could tank my career. So we need to put an end to this now, for good. For all our sakes."

25

RYDER

How the hell did we all end up in a situation like this?

I almost can't believe I'm standing here, having this argument. I also can't believe I watched a woman I care a hell of a lot about getting fucked from behind by somebody I used to think was my friend. I mean, he probably still is in a twisted, fucked-up way. If I were ever in trouble, I know he'd have my back. But not everything is a joke. Some of us learned that at a young age, but I guess he never got the memo.

Ash throws his hands in the air. Out of the three of us, he's the only one who's reacted yet. "Right. Once again, let's just pretend none of this ever happened and move on. Do you honestly think it's that easy? Or is this another game?"

"I would seriously appreciate it if you would stop acting like I'm some coldhearted bitch," she warns him. Her teeth are gritted, her face is red, and she's so goddamn hot. I don't know what to do with myself. The last thing I should care about right now is how hot she is – I mean, I'm still pretty pissed off and more than a little bit insulted. She was just with us last night, and today she's fucking Soren for the rest of the hotel to see. I can't help but feel like we mean nothing to her.

Like I mean nothing to her.

"Maybe you need to stop acting like one," I murmur. "I know that's not who you really are, but it's how you're acting right now."

The way her eyelashes flutter makes me feel like a piece of shit for saying it, even if it's something she needs to hear. "Is that supposed to make me feel any better?" Her chin trembles before she turns around to face the window. "Seriously. A coldhearted bitch?"

"He's not wrong," Ash mutters. Wow, for once he agrees with me.

"This is why it needs to stop." She wraps her arms around herself, and in the reflection in the glass I watch her close her eyes. "That is not who I am. But that's how I'm coming off, and I understand why. I don't know how to explain the way I feel. I know none of this is right, but when I'm with you… It's like there's nothing I can do to stop it. All of a sudden, I've got every excuse imaginable for being with you. It all seems completely normal and natural and right. And when it's over, I feel like this. Like I went and hurt somebody again. I don't want to hurt anybody, and I don't want to hurt myself. I don't know any other way to explain it."

"That's it? That's all there is? You get to make the decision and go back on it tomorrow?"

Something close to anger stirs in my chest and I want to grab Ash and tell him to knock it the hell off. The impulse is so strong, I can hardly resist it. He has no right to talk to her that way. He's hurting her, can't he see it?

Of course he can. That was the point. Because he's hurt, too. I know he would never admit it, but he is.

And so am I. The idea of never being with her again leaves me feeling sort of empty. Like there won't be anything to look forward to anymore. No, instead, I'll have to co-exist with her and act like nothing ever happened. Sit in her office with nothing but a desk in between us and pretend I don't want more than anything to clear the desk and throw her on top of it.

Can I do that? I can do anything if I have to. Do I want to? Hell, no. That's the last thing I want.

Does it matter right now? That's the real question. because Ash is right about one thing, it seems like she's the one calling all the shots. Making all the decisions. I guess in the end, she has the most to lose. We're not going to lose our jobs over sleeping with the team's therapist, but there's all kinds of ethics and shit on her side of things. So I guess yeah, the person with the most to lose should be allowed to make these decisions.

But the thing is, she's made this decision before. Look where it got us. I'm just as frustrated over that as anybody else. The back and forth, push and pull. Never knowing from one day to the next what the rules are this time. If I'm allowed to look at her a certain way, or touch her.

"I'm trying not to go back on my decisions." She usually sounds so strong and tough, smart and confident. I hate seeing her the way she is now — trembling, unsure of herself, weighing every word before she lets come out of her mouth. She's afraid to make a mistake. She's under pressure. That's the last thing I want for her.

I wish I had the words to tell her so. Maybe I could if it weren't for the other two people in the room. I don't know how to say something like that in front of them. It would be hard enough saying it alone. So all I can do is stand here like a coward, basically, while it feels like my heart's going to burst. I want to reach out and hold her and tell her everything will be alright, that nobody's going to hurt her, and that we're not going to make this any more complicated than it already is. Hell, I can't even promise that. It would mean speaking for people other than myself, and there's no point in it.

"This doesn't have to be so serious, you know." Soren shrugs when Ash and I look his way. "We're just having fun, right? Nobody gave anybody a ring or made any vows."

"You're right. We're all just screwing around." I can't believe it took me this long to see a solution. Well, a possibility. It's only a solution if everybody commits to it – and for all I know, it could be completely crazy. I could be talking straight out of my ass. "But what if we weren't?"

Now, all eyes are on me. I've never been much good at public speaking, so I don't exactly love the feeling, but this is more important than that. She is more important. "What if we quit screwing around and got together, instead?"

"What?" Harlow's brow wrinkles while her eyes dart over my face. "I don't understand."

"What if we finally got serious? I'm not talking vows and rings," I add, looking at Soren. "But what if we finally set ground rules? No more hiding. No more

secrets, no more lying. What if we were all...
together?"

"I still don't get it. What are you really saying?" she asks, taking a step closer to me.

Well, there's no going back now. I went and opened my mouth, and I can't take it back. There's nothing to do but push forward. "What if the only time you had sex with any of us was when we were all together?"

26

HARLOW

I'm pretty sure I must be hearing things. There's no way, right? He did not suggest what I think he suggested.

Considering the absolute shock etched all over Ash's and Soren's faces, I'm guessing they feel the same. "What did you just say?" Soren scratches his head, then tips it to the side. "All of us together?"

Poor Ryder. He looks like he'd rather swallow his own tongue than keep talking. "I mean what I said. No more sneaking around behind each other's backs. No more arguing over who gets to spend time with her or what we mean to her."

"Excuse me?" I raise a hand, gritting my teeth in a parody of a smile. "I do have a name."

"Sorry. Harlow." And for once, he's not being snarky or sarcastic. "We wouldn't have to argue over what we mean to Harlow. We can finally make this an arrangement instead of flying by the seat of our pants and getting pissed at each other. It's all a waste of time, anyway. And it's not worth breaking up our friendships."

Ash stares almost menacingly, calm and quiet, standing with his arms folded and his expression stony. The fact that he didn't shoot it down immediately – or worse, burst out laughing – tells me he might be considering it. Could that be true? Could he honestly entertain the idea?

How do I feel about it?

"It only makes sense," Ryder's speaking to all of us, but his focus is trained on me. "I mean, if that's what we all want."

"Let me get this straight." As usual, Soren is smirking like this is all a big joke — though the lack of laughter in his voice tells me it's more a look of uncertainty. "Would it be, like, a huge group relationship? I don't get where you're going with this."

"I'm not sure what part of this is so hard to understand." He throws his hands into the air, looking around. "I'm just saying, let's be honest with each other about it. If Harlow wants to be with us, fine. But let's be upfront about it. Instead of it being me versus you versus you —" He waves a hand, indicating the three of them, "It could be sort of a group arrangement. We all acknowledge we've got something going on with Harlow, and that's it. No more sneaking around, no more getting offended."

An arrangement. I can't pretend the idea isn't a good one. I'm sick to death of having to go behind people's backs and feeling even lower every time I do. Like a liar, like a cheater – which is funny, since I can't cheat on somebody I'm not seriously involved with. But that's how all of this makes me feel. And here's Ryder, suggesting an arrangement that could put an end to that.

"So what you're saying is, we could all continue having sex," I muse, "but we would all acknowledge that it's happening and not try to keep it from each other?"

"Yes — but more than that." He waves his hands, frowning. "I'm having a hard time describing what I'm thinking. It's all sort of barely thought out, anyway."

I can't get a read on Ash. He looks like a bomb just dropped on his head and he's still trying to figure out how to deal with it. Is there a tiny bit of disappointment involved, too? It would feel conceited to think so, but I can't pretend I don't see it. I don't know if he wants this to work or not.

How do I feel about it? Besides the relief of not having to go behind anybody's back, could I handle this? I won't pretend I'm not intrigued. I won't pretend it's not sort of exciting. All three of them at once? Who wouldn't fantasize about something like that?

This is more than a fantasy. These are real, live people who I happen to care about very much. I can't let myself get swept up in silly fantasies.

"Well, I'm in." Because of course, Soren is always ready for a little excitement. "I mean, it sounds good to me."

"Like it's that simple?" Ash looks downright gobsmacked as he studies his friend, like he's waiting for another joke when Soren looks completely serious for once.

"Sure. What's the point of getting all caught up in questions and stuff? That's a waste of time. I already know I like being with Harlow, and if that means sharing, I'm up for it." Though at the last second, his eyes go narrow. "One condition. When we're together, we're all together. The four of us. No sneaking around and trying to score a little extra credit, if you know what I mean."

"Honesty," Ryder agrees, nodding. "Yeah, we've got to have honesty. That's the point of this. So none of us feels like we have to sneak around behind each other's backs. We can make this an actual, you know… Arrangement. We're all adults. We can make this work like adults."

Still, Ash has kept his thoughts to himself. What is he thinking? If there's one thing he's good at, it's hiding his thoughts behind a stony façade. I don't want to push him – that's the last thing he needs when he's got so much on his mind. Still, my anxiety is starting to grow worse with every silent moment that passes.

It's Soren who does me the favor of challenging him. "Don't act like you're not thinking about it," he warns with a patented smirk. "Or that you don't have questions. Might as well get them out of the way now."

"Oh, I've got questions," Ash assures him. "For one thing, what about other people? Can any of us go off and sleep with somebody else? Or do we keep this exclusive?"

Right away, there's a distasteful feeling that stirs in me when I think about being with anybody else. I don't like it. And I don't want them thinking I'm the kind of girl who is going to sleep her way through the entire team. They're special to me, all of them.

It's Ryder who speaks first, shaking his head. "No. The way I see it, we're all friends with benefits here, but it's exclusive. If we decide to go ahead with this, we only sleep with Harlow, and she only sleeps with us. I think that's the only fair way to make this work so nobody feels left out or offended or whatever."

"Yes, I agree." Soren grins and even acts like he's wiping something off his hands, like everything's all set. "Well, that was easy."

"You don't speak for everybody," Ash reminds him.

"Of course, you would have to make things difficult," Soren retorts, rolling his eyes.

"I'm not trying to make things difficult," Ash snaps. "I'm just saying, some of us can't make up our mind with a snap of their fingers the way you obviously can."

"Maybe some of us don't feel the need to make things harder than they need to be," Soren counters with a shrug. "The way I see it, this is the best solution. Everybody gets what they want, nobody has to get hurt, and we're open and honest about it. Really, this is a best case scenario type of solution. If you'd get out of your own way, you would see I'm right."

Is he right, though? Is this the best case scenario for everybody involved? I know how I feel – and what a relief it would be to have a little honesty between us. But I'm only speaking for myself. I can't speak for Ash, who still looks troubled, even after Soren and his rationalizations.

Three men at once. I almost can't wrap my mind around the idea. Three men with big egos and a feeling they have something to prove. Three men who would rely on me to have their needs met the way they would meet mine. Can I handle that? Can I juggle all three of them and make sure none of them feels slighted or left out?

I'm not sure, but the way my skin tingles at the idea tells me I would love to try. After all, I have always enjoyed facing a challenge.

And this could be the most enjoyable challenge I'll ever come up against.

27

ASH

Is this a fever dream? Because otherwise, I can't understand why everybody seems so okay with this idea. I must be imagining it in my head. All three of us?

I'm not a prude. I generally don't give a shit what people do in their private lives. When it comes to mine, I have never backed down from a good time. But this? This is unusual, and that's putting it mildly.

All three of us, and Harlow.

What are my options here? Well, I can tell everybody how uncomfortable I am with the idea, but what does that make me look like? And for how long will I have to put up with Soren being an asshole about it? Because this isn't just me I'm concerned with. Nobody has said it out loud yet, but I get the feeling this is a package deal. All or nothing. If one of us says no, the entire arrangement falls apart. Granted, I don't owe anybody anything. I would like to see them try and make me feel guilty. It wouldn't end well for them.

But this could be my only chance at being with her. I don't want to pass that up.

So what, then? Do I swallow my discomfort and act like this is all fine? Nobody would ever call me the *go along and get along* type. I'm not used to sharing, not this way. When I think about sharing her – having to coordinate with these two over when we will be together, all that — something hot and irritating grows in my chest. I want her for myself. Is that selfish? Do I care? I'm not going to stand here and pretend to be thrilled, not even for her sake.

But it might mean having to put an end to this for good. At the very least, it would mean always asking myself who's with her. Who's touching and holding and kissing her. Whose name she's moaning. The idea of that makes me so angry, I can hardly think. I need to stop imagining it, or I might end up starting a fight over something that's only happening in my head.

"What are you thinking?" she would have to go and ask me that, wouldn't she? I need to turn away from her penetrating stare. She's got this way about her that makes it feel like she's looking straight through me. Like she can see what's going on inside my head. I don't want that. I've never been good at vulnerability.

"He's probably thinking of how he can keep you all to himself."

"Would you give it a rest?"

"Just let him think," Ryder snaps at Soren. "This isn't something you jump into without thinking about it."

"What's there to think about? I'm being serious." Well, that would be a first. Soren stands, and for the first time since this conversation started, he looks concerned. Not in a fake joking kind of way, either. "We know we have fun when we're together, and it's either that or be done with the whole thing. It doesn't take much time when you look at it that way. I know I like being with Harlow enough that I am willing to share her – if that's what she wants. Why screw things with overthinking? That's how you ruin something worthwhile."

The thing is, I see where he's coming from. He makes sense.

But that doesn't make it any easier to commit myself to this. I almost want to ask for more time. The night, maybe. We could come back to this in the morning.

But is Soren right? Am I overthinking everything? Could it be as easy as agreeing to the idea and going from there?

If she were anybody else, I wouldn't have to think too hard about it, but that's the thing. She isn't just anybody. And this is about more than fun. At least, it is for me.

There I was, thinking Ryder would be the obstacle here. He's the one who came up with this crazy idea. I thought for sure he'd be on my side, that we'd both be just as pissed after what we saw. I still can't shake the memory of how the sight of Soren taking her from behind made me feel. I went from flying high after last night to wondering what I mean to her. If I ever meant anything at all. I figured we had a good thing going.

Apparently, I'm not enough. And neither is Ryder.

There she is, trembling, practically swimming in what has to be Soren's robe. I guess they're a one-size-fits-all sort of thing – she looks adorable in it, and I sort of hate that she does, because I can't let myself get distracted. And I can't let the craving I have for her get in the way of my judgment. She's a craving I can't shake, the sort of thing that haunts a man's thoughts every minute he's awake.

But that doesn't mean I would want her all for myself. I'm not in love or anything like that. I just don't like being replaced without getting the heads up first. I wouldn't even want to be exclusive with her. I know that. I'm not kidding myself into thinking there's some deep, soul connection sort of thing here. She's special, yeah. So special I'm actually considering Ryder's insane idea. But I'm not in love. I'm not looking for a commitment.

Still, even though I know all of this, the thought of walking out of this room after saying no turns my stomach a little. It's that unthinkable. I want her again, and I'll want her again after that.

Do I want her so much, I'm willing to put my pride aside? Do I want her enough that I'm willing to share her with my teammates?

That's it. That's the problem. It took me this long, standing here and working it out in my head, to understand what's at the heart of my hesitation. I sit on the bed, bending forward and lowering my head into my hands. It's that I'd have to share with them. Not some nameless, faceless guy she's sleeping with. I'd have to see them every day. Work alongside them. Figure out how to co-exist. That's the tough part. I'm not that great at sharing in the first place. How do I share with them?

How do I not? Because as uncomfortable as it would be to see them every day and carry this secret, it would be ten times worse to know they resent me for ruining their chances of being with her. Either way, this is going to be tough. I might as well get laid in the process, right?

God, I'm actually considering this. I'm actually trying to talk myself into it.

I feel the weight of their unspoken questions, and it's enough to make my skin crawl while I grit my teeth in frustration. Do I have it in me to share? Can I promise myself I'm not going to fuck this up somehow?

"What are you thinking?" Harlow's voice is small, hesitant. Right now she's the complete opposite of the self-assured, accomplished woman I've come to know.

"What are you thinking?" I ask before lifting my head to look her in the eye.

"No fair." The corners of her mouth twitch like she's trying not to grin. "I asked you first."

"Honestly? I don't know." I scrub my hands over my face and sigh. "I mean, being with you is better than not being with you. And I don't want to be the one to ruin everything by saying no."

"Nobody's trying to force you into anything." Soren's frowning at me when I glance his way. "You know that, right?"

"For real," Ryder agrees. "There wouldn't be much point to any of this if one of us felt pressured."

"Yeah, I know."

"We would understand." Something tells me Ryder would not understand, and neither would Soren, but they're trying. I've got to give them credit. They're at least putting an effort into making it look like they're understanding.

"For what it's worth," Harlow whispers, "I'm willing to give this a shot. I mean, I'm curious. I know it would take communication and working together, but I think we could have a good thing here. Only if you're into it, though."

So she's into it. Well, why wouldn't she be? She gets to lie back and have all three of us worship her at the same time. There's really not much of a drawback for her.

It's obvious I'm not getting out of this room without giving them an answer. There's only one that seems to make any sense after looking at the problem from all angles. "Fine. Let's do it."

"Really?" It comes out as a squeak, and Harlow's eyebrows pretty much jump off her head, she's so surprised.

"What, did you think I would say no? I just had to think about it." Looking around the room, I shrug.

"I mean, it's better than feeling like we have to sneak around behind each other's backs. We'll make it work."

I only wish I knew how.

But I'm not going to sit here and pretend the idea of figuring it all out doesn't interest me more than a little.

28

HARLOW

Wait a second. Am I dreaming this? Can any of this be happening?

I don't even know how I feel about this idea, yet I am now facing the expectant stares of all three of them. I don't know what to think. I mean, I'd be an idiot for passing up this opportunity, wouldn't I? I already know how good it feels, being with them. They have shown me a whole new world, and not only when we're in the middle of fooling around. They've shown me what it means to be respected and wanted, really wanted. I now know what it means to be truly taken care of. Sure, they use me, but I want them to. And never, ever have they made me feel pressured. Annoyed, sure, but never pressured into doing what they want, when they want it. Just thinking about that makes my heart swell with gratitude and affection.

And I wonder how much better things could get. Is it greedy to imagine they could? To want more? Do I even care?

No, I don't think I do. I'm tired of caring about right and wrong, whether I'm a good girl or not. Aside from the job concerns – which are still very real – I'm learning to let go of *should*. It's an ugly word, anyway, and probably the root of most sadness and dissatisfaction. This idea that things *should* be a certain way, that people *should* be a certain way. It's not fair.

They only want me to be me. They want us to be together.

But all three of them at once? That's a lot of male ego to manage.

And let's face it, that's three times the likelihood of being discovered. Is the risk worth it?

Would I hate myself forever if I decide it's not?

"This is a lot." I sink onto the bed, then shake my head as Ryder moves closer like he wants to comfort me or something. "No, just let me think. I need to work this out."

"You don't have to make up your mind right away." Soren pretends not to notice the way Ash rolls his eyes. I know he doesn't mean it, really. He's impatient. I might even be flattered by that.

"We're all willing to take a chance on this," he points out.

"She has the most to lose, man," Ryder reminds him. "At least let's give her the chance to think it through, you know?"

Ash's expression softens. "I'm not trying to get you fired. You know that, right? None of us wants to hurt you in any way."

"I know that." I smile, because it's true. "But I can understand why you would want an answer right away, too."

"We'll have to be careful." Ryder strokes his jaw, pacing the room. "No screwing around at the arena. We'll arrange our times together in advance."

"So much for spontaneity," Ash sighs. When I give him a sharp look, he flinches and holds up his hands. "I'm just saying. I'm not trying to force anything."

"I know it's not ideal," I agree with a sigh. "But this is the way it's going to have to be if we have any hope of making this work. We have to be so careful. I like all of you enough that I'm willing to consider this crazy idea – I have to be sure it doesn't come back to bite me in the ass, though."

"Is that all you're worried about?"

I might as well be honest. These are men I'm considering starting a relationship with. We need to begin from a place of honesty. "To tell you the truth, I'm not sure I can handle all of you."

Right away, like magic, the three of them go from looking concerned and even sympathetic to downright full of themselves. "I don't mean that way. I can handle that. Jeez. I meant, I don't know if I can handle your needs otherwise. How do I keep you from feeling a little neglected, for instance. I want to make sure I give everybody the same attention."

"You're a sweetheart to think of that." Ryder's smile is kind, gentle. "And I can see why you would worry about it. But we're not babies."

"Are you sure about that?"

All of us scowl at Ash. "See, that's what I'm talking about," I tell him. "Your little quips don't do anybody any favors."

At least he looks contrite. "I'm busting balls. I don't even mean it."

I have to wonder. "I know it's not my business to tell you guys how to treat each other, but I don't want the tension and the negativity. If I know you're all behaving yourselves, so to speak, I'll feel a lot better about this. Not so guilty."

"I think we can all agree to that." I don't think it's an accident when Soren looks at Ash. "Right?"

"Damn. None of you has a very high opinion of me."

"That's not true. And I know Ryder can be just as much of a troublemaker." I turn his way, arching an eyebrow.

"I'll do my best. I'll turn over a new leaf. All the new leaves you want." He's not even kidding. I've never seen him look so serious, in fact. There's an intensity to him that I appreciate, even if knowing I am the cause of it is a little overwhelming. Like, am I enough to make a man want to change his ways? I still don't get what's so special about me.

"What about protection? Health and safety? I'm on the pill, for what it's worth."

"We've all got clean bills of health." Soren looks around, while Ash and Ryder both nod. "I'm sure you can find our full physical work ups and blood tests and all that."

"I'm not going to invade your privacy, but it's good to know." So that's settled. And with each question answered, a little more of my hesitation fades away. It's only the ethical, professional concerns that are in my way now. I can't dismiss those like they mean nothing. "I just want you guys to know if things ever get weird – if I act a certain way when we're in public, or if I think we need to back off a little bit because maybe somebody's acting like they're suspicious of us — I need you to understand it has nothing to do with you. I still have to be safe."

"Of course. And we'll all be careful, too. We'll keep our eyes and ears out." Ash looks so hopeful, it's almost enough to break my heart. He really wants this. They all do.

And so do I. It's stupid to think I could drop them, like I could forget them all at once. That's never going to happen. I care about them too much. This way, at least, there won't be the feeling of cheating on somebody whenever I'm with one of them and not the others. That idea alone is enough to push me toward accepting this offer.

"Okay." Why not? You only live once and all that.

Soren gets up from the bed with his hands extended, and I place mine in his to let him pull me to my feet. "You're sure?"

"Yes." It feels right. It feels good. "Yes, I'm sure."

"Why don't we seal it with a kiss?"

The way he says it makes heat stir in my core, but that's what he wanted. He knows exactly what he's doing.

He takes my chin and tips it upward so our mouths can meet. His kiss is tender, soft, sweet. Somehow, it still has the power to make me tingle.

"Hey, save a little for the rest of us." Ash stands by my side and I break the kiss with Soren so I can kiss him now. His kiss is sensual, long and slow. His tongue slides against mine, and we both groan while he buries his hand in my hair and holds my head still.

Once he lets me up for air Ryder takes his place, kissing me with more urgency, claiming my mouth. I can tell there's always going to be an unspoken competition among them. They're all going to want to be the best, because that's who they are. That's how they live. I'm not going to pretend the idea doesn't excite me – I'm trembling with anticipation by the time Soren unties the belt around my waist so Ash and Ryder can slide the robe over my shoulders and down my body. They're almost reverent, easing me into it, and by the time I'm standing naked before them, I'm aching with need.

"Somebody needs to touch me now, or I'm going to explode," I whisper, trembling a little as I lower myself to the bed. The bulges in front of my face tell me they feel the same way.

I bite my lip, taking in the sight of them before I lift my gaze. "So, who's going to be first?"

29

ASH

No, this is not ideal by any stretch. I don't share. I would still rather have her all to myself if I could, but I forfeited that opportunity when I agreed to this. I would rather have to share than never have her at all.

Right now, I don't give a shit about sharing. She's sitting there in all her naked beauty, her perfect tits rising and falling with every ragged breath. She's nervous, for sure, but she's also hungry. I see it in her eyes, in the flush on her cheeks and her tight nipples.

Nipples I reach for with my left hand while undoing my belt with my right. A soft smile plays over her mouth before she sucks in a breath when I touch her, playing with her tits while I drop my jeans. She eases my hand out of the way and does the rest for me, lowering my boxer briefs so my dick can spring free. With our eyes locked, she extends her tongue and runs it around my head until my knees threaten to buckle. I hear Ryder and Soren taking off their clothes, but the sound barely registers on my awareness while this woman teases me like only she can.

Fuck, I wish I'd had the chance to be with her alone. Just once. Just to have all of this for me and me alone.

The thought is swept away when she takes me in her mouth and sucks me in long, slow strokes. Wet, sensual, while I run my hands through her hair. "You're so good to my dick, baby," I whisper, making her moan in response.

But, of course, it can't last forever. My friends want their turn, and they take it, with Ryder, placing a hand on her shoulder to get her attention while stroking himself with the other hand. She grins playfully before plunging down on him. A minute of that, and she turns to Soren, standing on my left. I have to admit, it's hot, watching her pleasure them, hearing their reactions. I know how good it feels, how good she is. It's enough to make pre-cum drip from my tip, and she's quick to catch it on her tongue before she lies back, propping herself up on her elbows and spreading her thighs. I have to remind myself to breathe, seeing her like this. That knowing look in her eye – she understands what she's doing, and she feels powerful. That's all I want for her, especially when it always turns out so good for me.

None of us has to say a word. I drop to my knees and drape her legs over my shoulders, running my hands over her silky smoothness, lapping at her ankles and the insides of her thighs. Indulging myself in her – the taste, the scent, the arousal that intensifies the closer I get to her shaved pussy.

I part her lips and swipe my tongue over her pink, glistening flesh. She moans softly, running her fingers through my hair. "Oh, that's nice. That is so nice…" I look up across the length of her body to find Ryder and Soren indulging in her – caressing her, kissing her neck and her chest, lapping at her nipples. I don't know if she's talking to me, or to one of them, or to all of us. Even now, with my dick straining and dripping and my tongue buried in her heat, I can't shake the desire for her to moan just for me. I want to know I am the one making her tremble and whimper and beg for more. That I am the one who turns her into this sensual goddess, that I can make her forget everything she thinks she needs to be.

And it makes me work harder, sucking her clit, massaging her inside with one, then two fingers. Her hips jerk when I find her G-spot, and I work it. A surge of pride runs through me when her hips grind in time with my strokes.

"Yes… Yes, Ash…" I don't change a thing, doing exactly what she wants, giving her what she needs until her low, deep moans rise in pitch. A rush of warmth coats my chin as her muscles clench around my fingers, and I ride it out with her, forcing her to accept what I want so much to give. I need her to forget everything and everyone in favor of this. Us.

She comes down with a happy little sigh and holds her arms out to me. Ryder moves out of the way and I take his place, groaning when she takes me to her mouth again. "Returning the favor?" I ask with a chuckle that turns into a moan, and she responds by sucking harder than before. With more purpose. On the other side is Soren, who she strokes while she sucks me. Our eyes meet and I can't describe the energy that passes between us. More like an understanding. This is who we are now. It was never going to be a one-off sort of thing. And watching pleasure wash over him does something to me. It makes me surge in her mouth and move my hips while Ryder plunges in and out of her, holding onto her thighs for leverage. He rocks her body back and forth with the force of his strokes, but her ecstatic cries say she likes it. And that makes me like it, it makes me grunt and gasp and fight to hold on even when I know I can't. I'm too far gone.

Ryder pulls out quickly, shaking his head. "Don't want to finish yet." He steps back so Soren can take his place, and the look of pure bliss that lights up his face makes me cradle Harlow's head in my hand to fuck her mouth the way he's fucking her pussy. It should be me, dammit, I wanted it to be me, just me. And it never will be.

But somehow it's all right when he looks at me again, and again a silent message passes between us. If it had to be with anybody else, I'm glad it was him.

She presses her feet against the bed and meets his strokes, moving her hips, almost inviting him to take her harder. Watching her do them is a rush, like my own personal porn video. Only I'm not jerking off alone. It's her mouth doing the work for me, and every stroke takes me closer to the edge.

That's not how I want to finish, and I don't want sloppy seconds. "Quick," I grunt, pulling out of her mouth and practically shove Soren aside, so I can bury myself in her tight heat. God, she's so wet now, and her muscles are quivering like she came for one of them.

It doesn't matter. She's going to come again for me.

She does me the way she did him, her eyes locking with mine while she thrusts her hips upward to meet my strokes. "Yeah," I grunt, grabbing her hips. "That's right. Fuck me."

"Yeah…" she whimpers, nodding, while she works my friends with both hands and they fondle her tits. "You feel so good inside me." Soren cuts her off by plunging into her mouth but that's alright, because I like to watch her fight to handle him while every thrust I deliver takes her closer to the edge. She's losing control and it's because of me.

Which is why I add a thumb against her clit. She squeals around Soren and pulls back gasping. "My God! Oh, yes! Just like that, oh, please!" When Ryder taps her mouth with his dripping head she takes him inside, moaning around him.

"Fuck…" He closes his eyes, his head falling back while he thrusts into her mouth. "Fuck, yeah, you're gonna make me come." Her cheeks hollow in response and the intensity of her reaction threatens to send me over the edge — but no. Not until she comes for me. I grit my teeth and hold on, strumming her bundle of nerves in time with my deep strokes.

"Yeah," Ryder pants. "Yeah, that's it… oh, Harlow, fuck yeah!" He plunges in deep, staying in place while he comes. Her throat works while a low moan stirs deep in her chest. She's swallowing, and she likes it. Her eyes shine when she looks up at him, but that doesn't last long once Soren gets a hold of her.

"I'm going to come on your tits," he decides, stroking himself while she licks his head. "What do you think?"

"Mm-hmm." She closes her eyes and arches her back and fuck, she's close. So close. Clenching around me like a vice. "Oh, God, I'm... I think I'm... yes!"

I've never felt the satisfaction I do now, not even on the ice. Knowing I can work her body like this and make her come until her voice breaks and her juices drip down my balls. Watching as a flushed glow colors her body. There's nothing that could touch this.

"Mind if I join you?" Soren grins my way and nods and I pull out, fucking my fist in the last seconds before the rush overtakes me and I'm lost to it. By the time the first splash of cum coats her skin, he's coming, too. Once the ringing in my ears dies down, Ryder is already cleaning her off with a wet washcloth.

None of us says a word for a while. None of us has to. It's enough to lie with her—me on one side, Soren on the other, while her head sits in Ryder's lap. It's enough to touch and kiss her and exist in this world only the four of us share.

30

HARLOW

As much as I miss the Seattle weather, the old saying is right. There's no place like home. Even if nobody would ever mistake me for Dorothy — I can't sing a note, for one thing, though I wouldn't mind a pair of ruby slippers. I don't know if I could live on a farm, though.

My polluted stream of consciousness is evidence of growing exhaustion. Trying to work out these new combinations for Coach Kozak is proving to be an even bigger challenge than I imagined. I want so much to ease his worries since he's got enough on his plate, God knows. But trying to work out a solution for every possible contingency is a fool's errand, to put it mildly. I'm starting to confuse myself. There must be a better way to put this information together, something succinct, something easily accessible. He hasn't come straight out and told me he wants to see what I've come up with, but the meaningful looks he gives me whenever we cross paths speak volumes.

There's one positive in the whole situation, of course. I don't have the time to sit and obsess over the men I'm in a relationship with. Even using that word in my head makes me frown. Is that what we are? Are we in a relationship? What other word is there for it, I guess? An arrangement? That sounds a little too formal, and we are anything but. The memory of our night together makes my cheeks heat up, and I bite my lip to hold back a grin. As it turns out, that was the only night we were able to get together — all three of them were a little too beat up and worn out thanks to the rigors of training camp. Not that I mind it, really. I was more than a little sore, myself, just in a different way. None of them are exactly on the small side, and they're all very... eager to perform well.

In other words, I considered icing my pussy more than once.

But they were true to their word. If one of them didn't feel up to hanging out, then none of us did. And that goes for me, too. If I don't feel up to it, that's it. No coercing, no pleading. No making me feel guilty.

Kyle could learn a thing or two. I lost track of the number of times I finally gave up and agreed to sex when I wasn't feeling up to it, only to shut him up. God, why did I put up with that for so long? I didn't know there were men open and respectful enough to care about my needs, my wishes. I can't even say I would go back and do it all differently, knowing what I know now, because that experience made me appreciate what I'm currently living with so much more.

I just wish I could tell somebody about it.

That's the hardest part. Wishing I could tell somebody, anybody about all of this. How many times could I have used an outside opinion? How many times have I wanted to flat-out brag a little bit about how great the sex is?

How many times have I wished somebody could tell me I'm doing the right thing?

But I can't do it. Even Ruby, who knows me better than anybody, would look at me funny if I caught her up on what I've been doing in my free time. She's probably the freest spirit I know, but there are some lines even free spirits don't cross. I wonder how free and non-judgmental she would be if I confessed.

I wouldn't even blame her. Hell, half the reason I was so hesitant about getting involved with the guys was the stigma surrounding this sort of unconventional arrangement. A three-way is

Pucking Disaster

naughty enough. But three-on-one? That's when words like *insatiable* and *nymphomaniac* start getting thrown around. And those are the nice words. *Slut* is another one that's not so nice.

Not that I think Ruby would ever, ever use those words. but I've done my fair share of research into social conditioning and the effects it has on us whether we're aware or not. And there's no way she wouldn't judge me, even if it was only to herself, deep down inside. I wouldn't want to see the little crease in her forehead or the narrowing of her eyes. I wouldn't want to think she saw me differently.

And let's not even get into the ethical concerns. I'm sure she would remind me of all the different ways this could jeopardize my career. She's seen how hard I worked. She knows how many nights I had to excuse myself from making plans with her because I had a paper to work on or research to dig into. There were times when I wanted to give up – I didn't even tell Kyle about those times, because I had the feeling he would've supported me in the decision. Not for me, but because he wanted more of my time, more of my attention. And I get the feeling now, with the benefit of time and distance from the relationship, he felt threatened by my devotion to my work. He didn't like how seriously I took it.

But Ruby stood by me. She encouraged me. She reminded me during those low moments of how far

I'd come, and how much I would regret throwing in the towel just because I was tired and overwhelmed. And I always pushed through thanks to that.

I can only imagine it would seem like a smack in the face if I confessed I was ready to jeopardize that for some great sex. Hot, incredible sex that makes me feel wanted and cherished and adored.

But it's still just sex. And something tells me she wouldn't be very sympathetic.

The groan I let out when I stand and stretch after hours of going through my notes on each player is both one of fatigue and irritation with myself. I'm in the middle of what could easily be called a perfect situation — at least, a great one, one that would make me the envy of pretty much every woman I know if they heard about it. I want to be happy. I want to be able to enjoy it. But there're always strings attached, aren't there? Always a caveat. And the worst part is, I can't help but wish there weren't. I'm a grown woman, and I know there's no such thing as perfection, but why can't there be? Is it wrong to want to have my cake and eat it, too? I mean, what's the point of having cake if you can't eat it, right?

I am entirely too tired, and entirely burned out. I've been staring at the walls of my office for days, ever since getting back from Seattle last weekend. No wonder my brain is starting to go off in all sorts of interesting directions.

At first, I mistake the tapping on the closed door for an animal tapping on the window. That's how soft and almost tentative it is — if I were listening to music, I would miss it. When it rings out again, a little louder this time, there's no mistaking it. I can't think of anybody around here who would knock so softly, unless it's one of the guys trying to sneak in and see me when they ought to be working out. The idea of one of them creeping over here to steal a few minutes should flatter me, but all it does is make me grind my teeth and march over to the door, flinging it open. "What do you think you're—"

Anything else I was about to say dies in my throat at the sight of a teary-eyed, red-faced Corey. "I'm sorry," she whispers before running a hand beneath her bloodshot, swollen eyes. "I couldn't think of anywhere else to go, and I knew you were supposed to be back this week."

"Oh, my God. What happened? Come in." Right away I step back and pull her into the room when it seems like indecision has frozen her in place. This is not the girl I know. She's usually so put together, smiling, energetic. I've always chalked it up to her being physically active all the time. There's just a natural sort of bubbly energy that radiates from her.

Most of the time, anyway. Now she pulls a tissue from the pocket of her sweatpants and uses it to wipe her nose before sitting down on the sofa. "What is it?" I take the box of tissues from my desk and place it between us, taking a seat beside her. "What happened?"

Her chin quivers before she takes a deep, shuddering breath. "Oh, nothing. I just found out my whole relationship has been a lie, that's all."

A strange sense of déjà vu sweeps over me. "You don't mean…"

Her head bobs up and down. "I mean I found out Sean is cheating on me. And this isn't the only time."

31

HARLOW

It takes a minute for her to get herself together since every time she starts to talk or looks like she's about to, she gets choked up again. All I can do is sit back and wait, giving her space and time, even though curiosity is threatening to choke me. That, and the déjà vu that keeps tickling the edges of my mind. I've been in her shoes. Although Kyle and I weren't engaged. There's a difference between knowing we were about to be, and actually hearing the question and putting on the ring. A ring she's no longer wearing.

"I'm so sorry," she finally manages to whisper after going through a couple of tissues and half a bottle of water. "I didn't mean to come in here and blubber all over the place."

"You absolutely do not have to apologize." I pat her hand, feeling a little awkward – friends or not, this is an uncomfortable sort of conversation to have. I feel so sorry for her, since I can relate. Though I would feel sorry for her even if I couldn't. She looks like she's been crying for hours. Even her nose is raw and red from all the tissues she's been using, and I'm surprised she could drive with her eyes so swollen and bloodshot. Her clothes are rumpled like she either slept in them, or pulled them straight out of a laundry basket before putting them on. She's a mess, in other words.

"You know, it's not like I didn't have suspicions. I can say that now. I can admit it out loud. I had suspicions. He was away so much." Anger creeps into her voice before she runs her hand under her eyes again. "But he's a good liar. An excellent liar."

"Can you tell me what happened? You don't have to, of course. No pressure."

She lifts a shoulder, letting out a bitter chuckle. "The oldest story in the book. The naïve fiancé finds evidence on the idiot's phone."

Right away, she shoots me a guilty look. "I wasn't digging, I swear. I went to pay the electric bill, and I forgot the bill is attached to his phone number. So they sent a verification code via text to his phone. He was asleep. He got in late as usual, and I assumed it was because of work. Stupid me." Her voice breaks, and my heart threatens to break with it.

She sniffles before continuing. "Anyway, I grabbed the phone off the nightstand and unlocked it, and there was this app open, right there on the screen. I've never seen it before. Like, I didn't even know what it was for. But there were messages. Oh, God, so many messages in the inbox. He was using a chat app to talk to these other girls."

"Oh, no."

"I mean, months and months of messages. I didn't even have to look all that long — and I hardly read any of them. I just scrolled to see how far back they went. Some of them, he was talking to the woman for a year. A year! And it was always things like 'I'm in town until tomorrow, what are you doing for dinner'. Or 'last night was fun, I'll be back around in a few weeks'. And they would make plans. And sometimes..."

She releases a wounded cry and bends forward, covering her face with her hands. "Sometimes, they would send him pics, and he would send pics back. It was disgusting."

It's not easy, keeping my personal feelings out of my reaction. I need to remember this is Corey's problem, not mine. These are Corey's feelings being crushed, not mine. It wouldn't be fair for me to bring my own past into it. "I am so sorry," I whisper, and when I begin rubbing her back, she doesn't stop me. It's the least I can do.

"How could I be so blind? All this time, I kept telling myself there was nothing unusual about his schedule. He's busy, he works hard, he's ambitious." She lifts her head, almost giggling. "Can you believe that? I actually tried to make him out to be a hero, almost. As if there's anything heroic about what he did. But I was that determined not to see the truth."

"None of us wants to see the truth about something like this. You can't blame yourself."

"No, you're right. I blame him."

"Does he know you found out?"

"Oh, he knows." She lowers her brow and practically snarls. "He definitely knows."

"Where is he now?"

"Why the hell should I care?" Her face crumples. "I'm sorry. I shouldn't be snapping at you. None of this is your fault."

"It's alright. You're allowed to feel how you feel."

Her hands curl into tight fists. "I could kill him. How could he do this to me? I came out here because of him, to be with him. I told myself over and over to do everything I could to make us work. And I did. I tried so hard. Why am I not enough?"

"I know this sounds stupid and trite, but it's the truth. It has nothing to do with you."

"Come on," she groans.

"I mean it. I know this feels very personal, obviously. But what he chose to do was not a reflection on you. It's on him. He decided it was easier and more fun to sleep around and deceive you. This isn't because you fell short or because you could've done something differently. I know you well enough to know you gave it everything, because that's how you tackle everything in your life. You always give a hundred and ten percent. I mean, look at me. You pushed and prodded and almost bullied me into learning how to skate, right?"

She chuckles, then leans back with a sigh. "What am I supposed to do? I feel like my whole life is over. Everything I have, everything I've done, it's all tied up with him. How do I untangle everything?"

I guess there's no question of whether she wants to go back to him – not that I blame her one bit. I mean, it was bad enough that I found out Kyle was cheating on me with one woman. I doubt that was the first time, but at least I didn't have to face the evidence of so many encounters.

"One step at a time. That's all you can do. You've got to take it one step at a time. First things first. Are you staying at home, or is he?"

"Oh, hell, I couldn't live there now. Besides, the apartment's in his name – we only got it through his residency program."

I was afraid of that. "Okay. So where are you going to stay?"

"How do I know? I don't have anybody out here!" She reminds me of a scared little kid, which I guess she is in a way. She might look like a grown-up but right now she's terrified and wounded and the future is too dark and cloudy.

"That's not true. You have me. And I have a house with extra room. Plenty of room. And you'll be welcome there as long as you need it."

"Oh, no. No, I don't want you thinking I came in here just to—"

"I don't think any such thing." Frankly, even if I did, I wouldn't blame her. She needs a place to stay, and I happen to have a spare bedroom. From the way she makes it sound, I'm also one of the only people she really knows around here. She feels isolated, maybe more than I ever suspected. She's the sort of person who keeps the tough stuff buried deep down. She pretends everything's okay, because she has too much pride to do anything else.

"I don't want to impose on you." She sniffles and wipes her nose before tossing the tissue into the wastebasket. "My problems aren't your problems."

"Who said it would be an imposition? Really, it's obscene, wasting all that space on somebody who's stuck in this office most of the time, anyway. You are free to stay with me for long as you need to. Whatever it takes, you know? And if you want me to go with you to your apartment and get your things together, I'll do that, too. I don't want you to have to go there alone."

She lets out a sigh that seems to deflate her body. She must have been really worried about that part. If she's now so relieved. I'm glad I can help her feel that relief. I know too well how it feels to have the rug pulled out from under you all at once.

"We're going to get you through this, okay? I promise. I know it doesn't seem that way right now, but you're going to come out on the other side of this feeling better. You're going to build a life for yourself that you love. But it's going to take a little time, I won't lie." I find her hand and close mine around it, squeezing. "But I'm right here with you. For whatever you need, as long as you need it. You're not alone."

"I don't know what I would do without you." She throws her arms around me and squeezes tight. "Thank you. You're an angel."

"An angel?" I have to laugh softly at myself while hugging her back. "I'm pretty sure I am anything but."

32

HARLOW

"I feel so bad for calling off today's lessons."

"How often do you call out of work, anyway?"

She appears to think about it as we leave the kitchen and walk out to the pool, where we've already laid out towels over lounge chairs beneath an umbrella. This is the sort of day that calls for time spent by the pool with a pitcher of margaritas, which I carry in one hand while Corey manages the glasses and snacks.

"I actually can't remember the last time I took a day off when I was scheduled to work," she admits before dragging a baby carrot through hummus and popping it in her mouth.

"Well, there you go. Everybody deserves a day off every once in a while. And if there were ever a situation that called for it, it's this. Take it easy on yourself."

Once the drinks are poured, I settle in, while she stretches out in her white bikini with an unhappy sigh. "How long does it take for things to start to feel normal again?"

On one hand, I don't exactly love being the authority on how to deal with a cheater, but I have to remember how lost I felt when I was in the thick of things with Kyle. How much I could've used a shoulder to cry on. Ruby was terrific, of course – she always is – but there's something to be said for experience, too. Looking at somebody and seeing how they came out on the other side, intact, unbroken. I'm glad I can be that person for her, even if it's not easy dredging up the recent past.

"Really, there are still days when I wake up and I have to remind myself that things are different. Do you know what I mean? I still have dreams where I'm in my old apartment and everything is the same as it was. And I hate to say it, but sometimes those dreams are nice. Sometimes I miss the way things were – but then I remind myself that's only how I thought they were. Do you know what I mean? There's a big difference."

"Oh, I know," she murmurs, looking and sounding miserable.

"You have to forgive yourself," I remind her in a soft voice. "You didn't know, and there's nothing wrong with that. You trusted him, because you're a loving, trusting person. You thought you found the person you'd spend the rest of your life with and you were determined to make it work."

She takes a long sip of her drink, staring thoughtfully at the pool. "So is this what it was like for you? I'm sorry, I'm sure you don't wanna talk about it, but…"

"No, it's alright." After all, I can't hide from the memories. And pretending doesn't make anything go away. It doesn't change how I felt. "And yeah, it was like this. I saw him cheating on me in real time. I wouldn't wish that on my worst enemy."

"That is so awful. You don't deserve that."

"I don't think deserve has anything to do with it. And really, if I hadn't been following them around, I wouldn't have seen it. So I sort of got what was coming to me, at least when it comes to that night."

"Were you a total wreck after, the way I feel right now?"

"I felt just about as bad as I've ever felt in my life. You tend to go through all the little things and look at them through different eyes. You start questioning things. Was he lying about this or that, you know? That sort of stuff. It can drive you crazy."

"Gee. I have no idea what you're talking about," she mutters before laughing. "That's, like, all I've been doing. Questioning everything. Going back through memories with a fine-tooth comb."

"I'm sure that's only natural – but be careful. Don't punish yourself."

"I'm trying not to, I really am."

I take a long sip of my drink before opening part of my heart I've kept locked up for months. "We were supposed to get engaged, you know."

Her brows draw together like she's in pain. "Oh, I didn't know that. That's awful."

"Yeah, it was. It really was." My throat closes up a little at the memory, but I push my way through it if only for her sake. "I'd just finished defending my dissertation and we were supposed to go on vacation to Punta Cana. It was pretty much understood that while we were away, he was going to propose. I mean, he even had me show him different rings that I liked, so he would know what he was looking for. I really thought this was it. I figured by now, I would be planning the wedding."

"Oh, the wedding." She pinches the bridge of her nose, squeezing her eyes shut. "I don't even want to think about it."

"So don't. One thing at a time, right? You don't need to keep all of this on your shoulders at once."

"I know, but it is going to come up. Everybody knows we got engaged. Me and the hot shot doctor. A fairytale romance." I doubt she could sound more bitter or disappointed if she tried.

"They'll understand. Everybody will."

She doesn't look so convinced. "It's almost enough to make me…" She trails off, staring at her fingernails after draining what's left in her cup.

"Do you want another?" I offer, lifting the pitcher. She nods, thinking while I pour.

Finally, I have to ask, "Is it almost enough to make you want to change your mind and take him back?"

"In my weaker moments." She squints at me. "That sounds pathetic, doesn't it?"

"Not at all. Really," I insist when she rolls her eyes. "You're only human, Corey. It's totally natural to go through these feelings."

"He humiliated me. The last thing I should want is to get back together."

"Do you think you ever could? Like, if he promised to never do it again, would you believe him?"

She thinks about it rather than firing off a quick answer. "Honestly, in a weaker moment, I would want to take him back. Because this sucks."

"I know."

"And honestly? Would it sound awful if I said I might even want to forgive him if this were only a one-time thing?"

"Plenty of people do. You wouldn't be the first."

"That's not what I was asking. Would it be dumb if I did?"

"Sweetie, only you can decide that." I sip on my drink as she thinks it over, toying with her straw while she does.

Finally, she sighs and shakes her head. "All I can do is look into the future, and imagine how impossible it will be to trust him after this. It would be one thing if this were just one girl, one time. But it's gone on for so long. He's told so many lies. Even if he never cheated again, the damage has been done. I'd always want to second-guess everything he says."

"And that's no way to live," I point out.

"No. It's not. And I deserve better than that."

"You definitely do." I hold up my glass to her. "Just think. It could be worse. You could've found out about this later on – like, after the marriage, after having kids. It would've been a lot more complicated."

"Jeez, you're right. That's true." Still, she looks so unhappy. "I just have to get over the whole icky part now. Telling people the engagement's off. Telling them why."

"You know, you don't owe anybody an explanation."

"I know, but that's also easier said than done. You've never met my family. They won't let up until I tell them the truth."

"You did nothing wrong, though. You have nothing to be ashamed of. You're doing the best thing for you, remember."

"I know. It's easy to forget that, though."

"This is the first step toward getting over it."

"What was your first step toward getting over it?"

It's got to be the margaritas, otherwise I would never blurt this out. "I had a three-way."

I've never seen a person do a full-on spit take in real life — until now. "Oh, my God!" she chokes out after spraying the patio with margarita she just sipped through her straw.

"Sorry, sorry. I didn't mean to startle you!"

"You did? You really did?" Her eyes practically dance with excitement. "Who with?"

Red flag, red flag. "You don't know them. Just two guys I met at a bar."

"Oh shit! How was it?" This is more enthusiasm than she's shown since walking into my office a little less than twenty-four hours ago.

"It was... really good," I admit before laughing softly. "And it definitely helped me get over the feeling that I wasn't good enough, you know?"

Her smile fades a little. "I know."

"You are good enough. This wasn't your fault. Keep telling yourself that. You didn't make him do anything."

"I know... But sometimes I wish there were something I could do. I guess it's easier to think I could've been in control somehow."

I know all too well how that feels.

For a long time, we sit in silence, sipping our drinks, lost in our own worlds. Sometimes, all you can do is be there for somebody without saying a word.

33

HARLOW

Ryder: I need to talk to you.

"Dammit," I whisper at his message.

Sure, we haven't gotten together in that way since Seattle, but I sort of hoped they could all be mature enough to understand when I simply don't have the time to get together. I mean, I can't be available at their beck and call, no matter how much they want me to be.

"Who was that?" Like yesterday, we've spent most of today out at the pool. Having margaritas at our disposal certainly doesn't hurt — though I have to be careful with the amount I drink. I don't want to confess too much. It's one thing for Corey to think it was cool for me to have a three-way, but it would be another if she were to find out just who that three-way was with or how things have progressed since then.

"Oh, it's nothing." I put the phone aside, face down. No matter how I've tried to get it through to Ryder and the others that I'm busy and unavailable right now, they don't want to take the hint. Well, things aren't always going to be easy – I knew that already. Still, that doesn't mean I have to like the feeling of needing to explain myself.

It's not like I wouldn't enjoy getting together with them. I have needs, too.

But I can't drop everything just because they want it that way. Maybe it's good that they figure it out now, so there are no further misunderstandings between us. I am not theirs to use at their leisure.

"I finally called my mom when you were in your office this morning." Corey looks downright pained as she helps me gather everything from around the pool. It's nice to be out here, but there's only so much time we can spend before we both start to crisp up no matter how much sunscreen we use.

"How did she take it?"

"Well, it took a while, but she finally stopped coming up with ways to hurt him physically."

I shouldn't laugh, but I can't help it. "At least you have her on your side."

"Yeah, now all I have to worry about is whether she'll keep her promise to not go to the apartment and murder him."

"At least she's not right down the street or anything. It would mean getting on a plane or at least driving a long time. Not the kind of thing you can do on a whim."

"That's true."

"See, and she didn't even give you any trouble over breaking off the engagement."

"No, strangely enough, she actually sounded kind of proud." I'm glad to hear that. Especially when she looks so glad. I don't know why it is, but situations like this make people feel guilty. And they're usually the people with the least to feel guilty for.

"Well, that's great." What's also great is the cool embrace of air-conditioning when we step into the kitchen and close the door. I do love sitting out in the sun and working on my tan, but it's a treat to get out of the heat for a while. "Now, you know you have her on your side. And she won't be the only one, I bet."

"You know, he hasn't even had the guts to text me yet."

"At all?"

She shakes her head. "Can you believe that? He's such a coward. How did I never see that before?"

"Believe me, I know what you mean. I still don't know how I ignored it for so long." I pull a cold bottle of water from the fridge and hand it to her before taking one for myself. "I guess humans are good at ignoring what they want to ignore."

"That's the truth."

My phone buzzes again, this time from its spot on the counter. It takes everything I have in me not to groan while I go over to pick it up.

Ryder: I'm outside. Your car is here, so I know you are.

Oh, my. God. I'm going to kill him. My fist tightens around the phone and I would swear the room is starting to go red. Why does he refuse to take the hint? Hell, I'm not even hinting. I flat out told him I have things going on and will be busy for a while.

"I'll be right back." She looks intrigued, but says nothing, when I cross through the living room and out the front door. Sure enough, there's Ryder's car, parked behind mine. *God, give me strength.*

I'm careful to open the door just far enough to slip outside before I glare angrily at him. "What part of what I said to you was so difficult to understand?" I hiss. "I told you, I have things going on right now.

I'm sorry if that doesn't fit into your plans, but life happens, you know?"

"But you never said what's going on." His folded arms and tight jaw tell me he feels like the wounded party in this. "You're being pretty damn sneaky and secretive."

"Ryder, I don't know how to get this through your head. I don't owe you any explanations, just like *you* don't owe me any. Got it?"

"That's it? We're supposed to be okay with you blowing us off all week?"

"You are just as busy as I am," I remind him. "So don't put it all on me."

"Can you at least tell me what's going on? What's the big deal?" Then, he looks over his shoulder towards Corey's car. "And who is that?"

"That's a car, Ryder."

"I know you think you're being funny —"

"Oh, I wasn't trying to be funny at all. I'm angry. I don't appreciate being made to feel like I need to explain myself to you all the time. This isn't going to work if I can't have a life of my own."

He heaves a sigh like he's the one being grilled. I have to remind myself to be patient – this is a new situation for all of us. "I'm sorry, but you can't blame me for worrying."

"Worrying about what?" I whisper. She's not going to stay put for long. Every second we spend bickering ups the chance of her coming out here and learning too much.

"I'm worried you changed your mind. What do you think?"

"I didn't change my mind." And now I feel bad for being so angry, but really, does this warrant an in-person visit? Not to mention multiple messages?

"So what's the big deal then?" It's like he flipped a switch, and suddenly he's back to being suspicious.

"I have a friend staying with me."

"Oh, really? What's his name?"

"Don't do that. You know Corey. She teaches skating. I'm sure you've seen her around a hundred times."

"Yeah."

I drop my voice to a whisper. "She just broke up with her fiancé. She needs a place to stay. So I'm sorry, but I can't have you over here. She knows who you are. You get what I'm saying?"

"That's it? Really? Does your friend need you to be here twenty-four-seven?"

I can't believe this. "If I choose to be in my house all day, that is my decision. You don't get to decide when and where I spend my time."

"I just think it's a little convenient, that's all."

"Oh? Do you think helping a friend going through hell is convenient? Wow. We have vastly different definitions of that word, I guess."

My heart seizes at the opening of the door behind me. Looking over my shoulder, I find Corey peering out. "Oh. Hi," she offers, opening the door a little wider when she sees who I'm talking to. "Ryder, right?"

I'm glad I get to look at him in time to watch him react. His posture immediately changes — instead of that defensive stature, he loosens up, sliding his hands in his pockets. "Yeah, hey. How are you doing?"

"I've been better, but whatever." She waves it off, then bites her lip. "Sorry, I didn't mean to interrupt."

"Not at all." My posture changes, too, my spine straightening, my chin lifting. "If there's anything else you need to talk about, we can go over it in my office this week. Sound good?" *Please, be smart about this. Let it go for now.*

"Sure. Thanks. I didn't mean to bother you." He lifts his hand in a silent farewell before returning to the car without looking back. What a mess. At least I got to watch him realize I was telling the truth. We definitely need to have a talk about boundaries.

Though right now, something tells me I have another talk ahead of me. I can't imagine it seems normal, one of my patients showing up at the house out of nowhere.

I head inside, prepared to face whatever is coming.

34

HARLOW

"Real question, are your patients in the habit of showing up at your house unannounced?"

Well, considering the sort of questions she could be asking, I guess that's pretty tame. "Stupid me, saying they can ask questions any time they have a problem."

She waits until I'm in the kitchen, while she sits at the island, before clearing her throat. "You know, it's funny. One little thing can change, and all of a sudden you see everything differently."

"What do you mean?"

"I knew from, like, a psychological standpoint that the guys on the team are hot. I mean, you have to be blind to not figure that one out."

"Yeah, probably."

"But, I mean... He is really, really hot."

Wow. This suddenly got pretty uncomfortable. What's even more uncomfortable is the fact that I have to hide it, the immediate tightening in my chest. The rush of heat in my cheeks that makes me turn around and look through the refrigerator even though there's nothing I'm actually looking for. I can't risk her noticing my reaction, and I can't seem to control it, either.

"Don't you think so?" she prods.

I close the refrigerator door, shrugging. "Sure, of course. He's hot. Like you said, pretty much all of them are. Even the married ones."

"So, what's his situation?"

Crap. There I was, thinking the worst I could face after his sudden visit would be uncomfortable questions about our relationship. Why he showed up out of nowhere, all that. I didn't know it could get so much worse, so much more uncomfortable. "You're not asking me to share personal information, are you? Like, from our sessions?"

"Oh, God, no! No, you've got me all wrong." She shakes her head, giggling softly. "I'm saying, like, is he involved with anybody? Does he have a girlfriend? Is he looking for one?"

I make a time out signal with my hands. "Girl, you need to back up. You are barely two full days out of a serious relationship. You don't need to be thinking about becoming somebody's girlfriend."

"Fine, not girlfriend. Fuck buddy? Is that still a term people use?"

Oh, they do. Do they ever. "Wow. You... are pretty drunk," I remind her with a laugh. I mean, it's true. She drank most of a pitcher while I sipped on a single glass. No judgment – I know how she feels and what she's going through. And it's not like I made a lot of super healthy decisions in the immediate aftermath of my breakup. Case in point, Ash and Soren.

She giggles along with me. "Of course, I am. That's beside the point."

"Are you hungry?" Anything to get her off this train of thought. "I have that beautiful salmon filet I picked up from the store. We could have that with some rice, or quinoa. Maybe some pasta?"

"Sure, whatever you're in the mood for." She sits with her chin propped up on one hand, tapping the nails of her other hand against the countertop. "I bet I could have some fun with him."

You could. I know from experience. "Just say no to rebound sex."

"You had it, didn't you?"

"For one thing, it was more than a week after the breakup."

"Oh, so there's a time limit I have to hit?"

"I'm just saying. You need to take care of yourself right now." For the record, I would tell her the same thing no matter who she was lusting after. It's different for her, too, since she was actually engaged and planning the wedding.

Or am I only telling myself what I want to believe?

"I know, I know. I'm not saying I'm going to throw myself at him tomorrow or anything like that."

"That's good."

"Maybe next week, though." She laughs when I groan in dismay. "Relax. I'm only kidding around."

"I know. Sorry. I guess I'm a little defensive."

"How come?"

"Oh, you know." I try to wave it off, but she's not having it.

"No, I don't know. That's why I'm asking." Her face falls, and I'm sure she's seeing right through me. It was only a matter of time. "Oh, gosh. Is he some kind of psycho?"

"No!" The idea cracks me up, and a little bit of my laughter is relief. I am feeling too guilty, paranoid. I have to stop jumping to the wrong conclusion all the time, or I'm going to drive myself nuts.

"So he doesn't, like, have a collection of dead bodies in his basement?"

"I mean, he could." I lift a shoulder, giggling. "We never covered that. Maybe that should be a question I ask during my first session with a new patient."

"Okay, that's good to know." She's chewing her lip when I glance her way, and the serious look on her face makes my heart sink. I can't let myself get too defensive and wrapped up in this, and I know it. I wish somebody would tell my heart.

"Are you alright?"

"Me?" I take the salmon from the fridge and set it on the counter before pulling a pot from a cabinet. "Sure, I'm fine."

"You seem a little... short, all of a sudden. Did something go wrong with Ryder? I know, you can't give me specifics."

Take it easy. You're being obvious. "It's nothing like that. I guess I'm a little annoyed that he thought it would be okay to show up here. We need to have a discussion about boundaries, and I'm not looking forward to it."

"Yeah, I guess that would be uncomfortable." She pretends to mop sweat from her forehead. "I thought you were mad at me for a minute there."

"Why would I be mad at you?"

"You sounded sort of…" I'm filling the pot with water when her gasp grabs my attention. "Oh, my God. I'm such an idiot."

"Why are you an idiot?"

"Because it's obvious something happened between you two in Seattle."

It takes serious concentration to keep a grip on the pot and not dump it all over the sink. "Wow. Talk about jumping to conclusions."

"Come on. This is me you're talking to." She looks like she's ready to climb over the island, she's that desperate to get information. I'm surprised there isn't saliva dripping from her lips, she's so hungry. "You know I wouldn't tell anybody. Did something happen with him? Is that why he showed up here?"

It would be so easy, wouldn't it? Unburdening myself. It would mean finally having somebody to talk to – at least, when it comes to Ryder. One out of three isn't bad, right?

No, because it would be impossible to talk about him and exclude the other two members of our makeshift relationship. Besides, ethics or no ethics, this would be bad enough if it were only Ryder I was sleeping with. I could still wreck my whole life if I got found out.

In other words, there won't be any quick, easy way out of feeling like I am very much alone in all of this. No spilling my guts to make myself feel better.

"Nothing happened." She looks anything but convinced when she leans back a little, squinting at me. Sizing me up. "I'm serious. Nothing happened."

"But you have a crush on him, don't you?"

"No." I shake my head harder when she smirks. "I really don't. Right now, I'm more concerned about you."

"You know I was only kidding around, right? I'm not going to run off and sleep with the first guy who comes along. Not that there's anything wrong with that," she adds right away, holding up both hands in front of her. "More power to you, but that's not my thing."

"I didn't take it that way. Don't worry."

"Still…" She wiggles her eyebrows. "It's sort of nice to notice guys again, and not feel guilty about it. Can you believe I actually used to feel guilty? Meanwhile, he was out there doing whatever he felt like doing."

It might make me a bad friend, but I'm glad that she's changed the subject. I'm not sure how many more lies I can tell before I get caught.

35

HARLOW

On one hand, it's nice to not be alone. Having somebody in the house, somebody who happens to be a friend, is a welcome change. Even though Corey is emotional at the drop of a hat, she's somebody to talk to – and honestly, she's someone to take care of. I like taking care of people. I haven't had nearly enough of a chance to do that lately since life has been such a whirlwind. And with training camp getting in the way, there was no time for my usual sessions with the players. So it's sort of nice, knowing I can help somebody feel better about what they're going through.

On the other hand, I'm still fielding phone calls and texts from the guys. It's not like I don't want to see them – it's been over a week since the last time we

Pucking Disaster

were all together, and I'm just as human as anybody else. They aren't the only ones with needs.

How much of a jerk would it make me if I went out for a little while to see them? I doubt there would be any time to have more than a conversation, but I'm starting to think it's necessary that we have it. Ryder has gotten off my back, but that's probably because he came here and we had it out. The other two, not so much. Hence the way they refuse to leave me alone.

But what do I do with Corey? And what excuse do I give her for needing to leave?

"No, thanks." She shakes her head at the offer of brunch late Sunday morning, once she finally drags herself downstairs and into the kitchen. Grief is not a linear thing, and that includes grief over a broken relationship. It was fine yesterday to sit around and drink too much and vent, but today is a new day. A different story. Dark circles under her eyes and her raw nose tell me she's done some crying.

"Some toast, at least? You need to get something in your system." I slide a glass of fresh squeezed orange juice her way. "Drink up. It will make me feel better." She almost grudgingly takes the glass, but at least she drinks what's inside.

"I'm sorry I'm such a mess."

"You are not a mess. And you don't have to apologize."

She looks out toward the pool, frowning. "I don't know if I could do that again today, no offense."

"Don't worry about it. We can hang out here in the house. Maybe we'll watch some movies or catch up on some TV."

"Yeah, that's not a bad idea." But she's chewing her lip when I look her way. "I'm not trying to keep you locked up here with me. It's beyond sweet that you're letting me stay with you, but you have a life of your own. I'm sure you have other things to do."

Or other people. "Nothing that's more important than you."

The buzzing from my phone tells a different story. "Are you always blowing up like this?" she asks when I pick it up and see who messaged me.

"Yeah, I'm the most popular girl I know." Turning the phone over, I find a message from Ash.

The guys are coming over to hang out in a little while. We need to see you.

"Is everything okay?"

I look up from the phone, surprised. "Sure."

"You didn't look that way just now. You looked sad."

Once again, the urge to confess everything is almost overwhelming. I hate sneaking around. I hate lying. But it would be immature and childish to spill my guts. I don't need the possible repercussions, no matter how much I trust Corey. She could easily spill the beans without meaning to.

"Not sad. It's just a friend of mine asking if I can stop by. I haven't seen them in a while." *Liar, liar, pants on fire.*

"You should go. No, I mean it," she insists when I shake my head. "I'll feel a lot better if you do. Not so guilty."

"Have I made you feel guilty at all?"

"Of course, you haven't. That doesn't mean I don't feel it anyway. This is all hard enough to deal with. I don't need the guilt, too. And I'm not good company." She gestures toward the TV in the living room. "I can figure it out. And there are some shows I want to catch up on."

I feel like a total jerk — at the same time, my pulse is starting to race in anticipation as I head out. I need to calm myself down, though. I'm not going over there for sex. I'm going over to have a talk.

So what if all of our talks usually end in sex?

"Oh, look here. She's still alive." Ash's voice trips with snide humor when he catches me walking in through the gate leading to the backyard.

"Don't be a smart ass," I retort. "Ryder could've told you that himself. He's the one who showed up at my house yesterday unannounced."

Whoops. Ryder shoots daggers at me before shrugging. "I really wanted to see her. It's not like I was trying to start anything without you guys."

"Yeah, right," Soren mutters, though he's smirking. Either he believes him, or he doesn't see the big deal. Sometimes his carefree attitude makes me grit my teeth, but at times like this, I am beyond grateful for it.

"Oh, you didn't tell them? Thanks a lot. I could've saved myself a trip." Then I shrug and tell them about Corey and how she's staying with me. "I feel like an ass for leaving her by herself. But I wanted to see you face-to-face so you know I'm not lying or anything. The timing is awkward, that's all. But it has nothing to do with you guys."

Then, because I told myself I would, I straighten my spine and give all of them a stern look. "And while I'm here, I would like to talk about boundaries. If we're going to get through this without anybody finding out our secret, I can't have you showing up to my house at random times, unannounced. I need you to respect that I have a life of my own. Can you please promise me that?"

"Well, since only one of us was dumb enough to go to your house in the first place..." Ash glares at Ryder, who shoots a dirty look right back because he's Ryder and that's what he does.

And it's all pretty tiresome from where I'm standing. "It's a simple question I'm asking. Can we please agree there shouldn't be any unannounced, unplanned visits?"

"That sounds good to me," Soren agrees in his usual casual manner. "Do you want a burger?"

I swear, I could get whiplash from the sudden change of topic. "Excuse me?"

"A burger. You know, usually made of beef, but sometimes turkey or, God forbid, vegetables?" He even pretends to eat one, raising his cupped hands to his mouth and taking a big bite of air. "They're usually pretty tasty."

Even though it makes me giggle, I have to stay firm, "I can't stay. I already told you that."

"Come on. One burger? That won't take long." He begins walking toward me, making me back up as soon as I recognize the gleam of mischief in his eyes.

"Settle down," I urge him, aware of how close I'm getting to the pool. Closer with every step. "That's not what I came here for."

"Come on," he cajoles, winking at Ash. Suddenly I'm being approached from two directions, both of them closing in on me with the pool at my back. "Just a few minutes. It won't take long."

"I'm warning you…"

"Of what? What are you gonna do?" Ash flashes a wicked grin, and I barely have the chance to drop my purse on the patio to save what's inside before both of them tackle me, forcing all three of us into the pool.

"I'm going to kill you!" I shriek as soon as I surface, running my hands over my face to push my hair out of the way. "How am I going to explain this to Corey?"

"A brief storm?" Soren suggests before reaching for me. I manage to move out of his grasp, but Ash catches me, wrapping his arms around my waist and nuzzling my neck.

"It's been torture," he murmurs in my ear, all breathy and needy. "Wanting to be with you. Missing you." Every word, every touch of his hands, makes it harder to remember why I came here, and the promise I made to myself to keep things brief. And to keep my clothes on.

Ryder sits at the edge of the pool, his legs dangling in the water. "Here. I'll help you out." He holds out his hands and tries to keep a straight face but fails miserably.

"Yeah, right." Ash only holds me tighter, shaking his head. "She's all mine."

"I don't remember saying I belong to any of you," I remind him.

Ash's mouth finds my neck, while his hands find my breasts. "Say the word, and this is over for now," he growls. My resolve is fading fast by the time Ryder pushes off the edge and starts making his way over to us. When he reaches me and takes my chin in his hand to tip my face upward, Soren is next to me, nibbling my ear. Ash runs his tongue along the side of my neck.

"Go ahead," Ryder invites. "Tell us to stop."

That's the thing. I know they would.

But I know I don't want them to.

"Stay for a little while," Soren breathes into my ear, while Ryder teases my mouth with his tongue and his lips, nipping and nibbling, until I have no choice but to melt.

I have no choice at all. My body and my heart won't allow it.

I'm theirs – and that's all I want to be.

36

HARLOW

This time, we don't even make it into the house. Is it the water heating up, or is it my body? It has to be the hands all over me — my legs, my butt, my breasts. Every touch is like another log on the fire, threatening to build what started as a simple blaze into an inferno. I'm helpless against it as they peel one layer after another from my trembling body, while I do the same to them, suddenly ravenous for the touch of their skin, for the feel of their muscles, as they move over me, under me, inside me. Nothing else will do. I need them, now.

One after another, they take turns kissing me, and I accept their kisses gratefully, moaning into their mouths while they take their time exploring me. Only once does common sense knock at the back of my head, forcing me to open my eyes and look around.

Ash notices and turns my face toward his. "We're safe," he whispers, rubbing his thumb over my lips. "The neighbors on both sides go away every weekend and don't come home until after dinner. There's nobody to see us."

Something about the idea of doing it out in the open gets me hotter than ever, so hot I cry out in a mixture of pleasure and agony when Soren's fingers find my swollen folds underwater. It's so good I think it might kill me. I don't know what to do with the intensity of the desire burning me alive.

"See?" Ryder asks. "You wanted this just as much as we did." I would tell him there was never any question about that, but Ash's tongue is in my mouth and I'm already close to coming. How can I help it with so many hands all over me, touching my most intimate places, stroking me just the way I like it? They've been paying attention, obviously, and they know just what I need.

And they are so eager to please.

I rock my hips, grinding against Soren's hand. Ryder takes my nipples between his fingers and tweaks them, flicking the tips before ducking underwater and using his tongue, instead.

"Let's try this." I let out a yelp of surprise when Soren takes my legs out from under me, but the hand he places under my back to support me leaves me floating on the surface in blissful abandon. Ryder lowers his head to suck my nipples while Soren continues working my clit with his thumb. Here I am, completely at their mercy and feeling completely taken care of. It's as close to heaven as anything I can imagine, wave after wave of the sweetest pleasure rolling over me while Ash holds up my head and whispers in my ear.

"You are so fucking hot," he growls before tonguing my earlobe. "So hot, so perfect. I can't wait to fuck you. There's nowhere I'd rather be than deep inside you, Harlow. I wanna feel you grip me tight. I want your juice to coat my balls. Do you want that?"

"Yes!" I shout, going stiff in the last seconds before the wave breaks. Close, so close…

"Then come for him," he whispers. "Come like a good girl, and you can have our cocks."

"Oh, God! I am – I'm coming…!" And then I do, my back arching as the most incredible feeling of pure, sweet relief crashes into me and there's nothing I can do but moan helplessly again and again until it passes and I come to, safe in their arms, still floating, still supported.

And still hungry. Now that Ash has put the image in my head, nothing else will do. "Let's get out of here," I manage between gasps for air. We barely make it to one of the lounge chairs, which Soren covers with a towel before I lie down on my back. Right away, Ash is between my spread thighs, sinking deep before I can take a breath.

"Fuck, yes," he whispers, closing his eyes like he's adjusting to the sensation.

"Hold on, man." Ryder sits me up partway and adjusts the back of the chair so my head is elevated – and at eye level with his crotch. "Give us a chance to get set up."

Ash shakes his head before pulling his hips back and driving deeper. "No way. No chance."

Ryder pulls his erect dick from his shorts and runs his head over my mouth before I take him inside all at once, savoring his moans just like I savor the taste of his excitement hitting my tongue. Soren caresses my neck, my breasts, before I turn my head to give him the same treatment.

And all the while, Ash moves inside me, taking me hard, almost rough. Soon the chair is scraping over the concrete under it.

"Take it easy." Soren pulls him back by the shoulder and Ash leaves me, still hard and glistening thanks to the juices that are flowing from me. Soren takes his place, lifting my legs and bracing them against his chest.

"Have you tasted yourself?" Ash asks before sliding into my mouth. There's something so incredibly hot and dirty about it, I find myself running my tongue over him like I'm licking him clean.

"Fuck, that's hot," Ryder groans, wrapping my hand around his shaft. I stroke him the way I'm stroking Ash with my mouth and loving every second of it – their sighs and their moans, the way we work together so easily.

"Can you come for me again?" Soren asks, and I let Ash fall from my lips to watch him grit his teeth, fighting to hold on.

"No way. You always get to feel her from inside when she comes. Give me a chance."

When Soren glares at Ryder, I shake my head. "Let him. I want you to come in my mouth." Who am I? What have I become? These words would never have come out of me before, but then I would never have fantasized about anything close to this before now. Drying off in the sun, being used and using them for all the world to see. Even a slight possibility of being discovered heightens everything.

"Oh, you better be ready," Soren mutters when he stands, while Ryder takes his place.

"Roll over," Ryder grunts before helping me do just that, until I'm on my knees with my arms wrapped around the back of the chair. it's so nice this way, the angle letting him go deeper while Ash and Soren stand in front of me so I can take turns sucking them. I'm so excited, I start matching Ryder's strokes, moving up and down.

"Oh, yeah," he groans, digging his fingers into my hips. "Fuck yourself on my cock. Make yourself come."

I'm going to. Nothing short of a bucket of ice water poured over my head would stop me at this point. Between the way he fills me and the way Soren can't help but fuck my mouth, I'm rocketing toward another orgasm.

"Are you ready for me?" Soren grunts before losing his rhythm in a flurry of furious thrusts that leave me gagging. "Here it comes…!" And then he fills my mouth with the taste of him, burying himself against the back of my throat as he does. I swallow every drop before he pulls out with a satisfied sigh.

Ash quickly takes his place, while Ryder goes from fucking to rutting like an animal, taking me so hard I cry out in surprise and pleasure. But Ash clamps his hand around the back of my head, silently demanding. He won't let me let him go.

Every part of me is lit up, tingling, hot. The rush of complete abandon is like a drug and I chase the high, giving myself over to it, giving in to my most filthy fantasies. Letting go.

Ryder slams deep one more time with a long, loud grunt that almost drowns out Ash's groans of satisfaction as he comes down my throat. A moment later, the warmth of Ryder's release coats my lower back.

And me? I'm in a haze, trembling and shaking and moaning helplessly when bliss pulls me under the surface and leaves me floating.

"Fuck, it's so much better when you come on me." Ryder uses a towel to wipe my skin clean then helps me lie down on my side before adding, "I won't complain, either way."

Ash crouches beside me and brushes hair away from my temple before planting a kiss there. "What do you think about going inside for round two?"

I should've known I wouldn't get out of here any time soon.

But like Ryder, I'm not complaining.

37

HARLOW

Either I'm going to win an award for this, or I'm only imagining how cool it looks. Like in that movie A Beautiful Mind. It might look like a masterpiece to me and end up being nothing more than red string crisscrossing over meaningless nonsense.

But this layout makes the most sense. After days spent toying with different ways to present a mountain of information, Corey helped me see the light. "Think of them as interchangeable pieces in a game, and each player is in a different category. Lose one, put another one in their place."

It was simple to the point of near stupidity—stupidity on my part, not hers—but it finally broke me free of the mess I had made in my head. I've always had a talent for overcomplicating things.

Suddenly, everything was clear and I knew what I needed to do.

Now, standing in my office along with Coach Kozak, I'm wondering how clear it really is. He doesn't look too convinced, stroking his stubbled jaw and screwing his face up like I just asked him to complete a complex calculus equation.

"I know it's confusing," I offer after way too many silent moments pass. "It's a lot of information." Even I think so, and I'm the one who put it all together.

Approaching the board, I explain, "As you can see, I've laid everything out here on these sticky notes. There's a note for each player. We can switch them out according to whichever player moves in or out of the lineup, depending on how the contracts shake out."

I have to say, stepping back from the enormous whiteboard and the colorful Post-It notes, that I'm pretty dang proud of myself. Having the evidence of my hard work laid out in front of me is pretty neat. It's tangible proof of the effort I've been putting in.

And when Coach Kozak grins after taking his time looking up and down the board, I can release the breath I was holding. "I knew you were good, but this is masterful."

"Okay, okay," I warn, laughing. "Don't give me a big head, now."

"But it's true. This is exceptional work. I can tell you put a lot of thought into how you could make it all make sense."

"I did," I admit. "I'm pretty sure I went a little off the rails while I was working it all out. This way made the most sense. So now…"

I go over to the board, where I've color-coded the players based on their strengths. "Let's say we lose Ryder. We can take Danny here and pop him in Ryder's place, since Danny's strengths are relatively the same. Or if it's Soren, we can still use Danny, but Soren carries so much of the weight in the second line, we might put Ryder in his place, and still use Danny to cover Ryder's position."

"It makes sense. It really does." He pulls off one of the sticky notes and studies it. "How long will these keep sticking?"

The fact that that's his first question makes me burst out laughing. I must have done a better job than I imagined if his biggest concern is the lifetime of a sticky note. "I don't know. We could always get a cork board and use pushpins. That could be a better long-term solution."

"This is invaluable information. Of course, I need some time to consider all of this." He reaches out to offer an awkward pat on my shoulder that means the world. "Well done."

"Thank you. I hope it helps ease your mind a little." I sink into my chair, grateful that I passed the test with flying colors. "I know how stressful this must be, but at least training camp went well and everybody came out of it in good shape."

When his face falls slightly, I get the feeling I reminded him of something he's not happy to report. Right away my walls go up. "Speaking of which, there isn't so much hanging in the air anymore. I have some definite news on the contract situation."

A chill ripples down my spine and all of a sudden, my heart's pounding. "Oh? I guess that's a relief, knowing for sure." I pick up the water bottle on my desk and force myself to sip it slowly, hoping to calm myself down so he doesn't think I've completely lost my mind. I can't believe how much is riding on this.

Whatever he says, I can handle it. Even though the idea of being without any of them makes me hurt inside. I hate the idea. They drive me crazy, but it's a craziness I chose, isn't it? Because I guess there's part of me that likes it.

Coach stands back from the whiteboard, hands in his back pockets. "Yes, I think we will be able to cover the deficit. It might get a little hairy at first, but we'll make it work. They're playing and acting as a team. They'll do what needs to be done for the team, even if it means hustling a little harder for a while."

Be careful. I can't make it look like I care too much. "So, what are we looking at? Who are we losing?"

"It won't be forever," he reminds me. Maybe he's reminding himself. "Just a few games at the beginning of the season in October."

I'm going to scream if the tension that's wrapped itself around me gets any worse. "But who?"

"Right now, it's looking like Ash and Soren are both definite. There are a few others in the mix, but they are the only two the Orcas practically fell over themselves to snap up. I'm looking forward to giving them the good news, but there are still details that need to be ironed out. Let's keep it between us until I give you the go-ahead. They might need to work on some mental block issues before heading up there."

All I can do is nod, forcing a happy smile while dread settles over me.

Both of them, gone at once and with no guarantee of how long.

How are we supposed to handle that?

How am I supposed to handle it?

THANK you for reading Pucking Disaster! The stakes and the drama get ratcheted up in the next installment - PUCK ME

A SECRET RELATIONSHIP with three professional hockey players who aren't exactly great at sharing the same woman is a difficult thing to balance…

ASH AND SOREN are about to leave for Seattle and the four of us need sometime to connect. They surprise me with a lake house rental where we can drink wine, have lots of steamy nights and fall even more in love with each other.

. . .

When they leave, our foursome is torn apart and Ryder and I are just not the same. But when we start to spend more and more time together, we realize just how much we are falling for one another.

Keeping this why choose relationship a secret has been a challenge and I'm tested when my friend Corey finds out that I am finally seeing someone.

Given that I'm the team's psychologist, no one can ever know that I'm dating three pro hockey players at once and we're in love…but all of that is about to change.

What happens when we get close to being exposed? What happens when our love is tested?

Also, if you never read the prequel, One Pucking Night, check it out here and see how Harlow first got into this sticky situation.

ABOUT CHARLOTTE BYRD

Charlotte Byrd is the bestselling author of romantic suspense novels. She has sold over 1.5 Million books and has been translated into five languages.

She lives near Palm Springs, California with her husband, son, a toy Australian Shepherd and a Ragdoll cat. Charlotte is addicted to books and Netflix and she loves hot weather and crystal blue water.

Write her here:

charlotte@charlotte-byrd.com

Check out her books here:

www.charlotte-byrd.com

Connect with her here:

www.tiktok.com/charlottebyrdbooks

www.facebook.com/charlottebyrdbooks

www.instagram.com/charlottebyrdbooks

Sign up for my newsletter: https://www.subscribepage.com/byrdVIPList

Join my Facebook Group: https://www.facebook.com/groups/276340079439433/

Bonus Points: Follow me on BookBub and Goodreads!

- amazon.com/Charlotte-Byrd/e/B013MN45Q6
- facebook.com/charlottebyrdbooks
- tiktok.com/charlottebyrdbooks
- bookbub.com/profile/charlotte-byrd
- instagram.com/charlottebyrdbooks
- x.com/byrdauthor

ALSO BY CHARLOTTE BYRD

All books are available at ALL major retailers! If you can't find it, please email me at charlotte@charlotte-byrd.com

Somerset Harbor
Hate Mate (Cargill Brothers 1)
Best Laid Plans (Cargill Brothers 2)
Picture Perfect (Cargill Brothers 3)
Always Never (Cargill Brothers 4)

Tell me Series
Tell Me to Stop
Tell Me to Go
Tell Me to Stay
Tell Me to Run
Tell Me to Fight
Tell Me to Lie

Tell Me to Stop Box Set Books 1-6

Black Series
Black Edge
Black Rules
Black Bounds
Black Contract
Black Limit

Black Edge Box Set Books 1-5

Dark Intentions Series
Dark Intentions
Dark Redemption
Dark Sins
Dark Temptations
Dark Inheritance

Dark Intentions Box Set Books 1-5

Tangled Series
Tangled up in Ice
Tangled up in Pain
Tangled up in Lace
Tangled up in Hate
Tangled up in Love

Tangled up in Ice Box Set Books 1-5

The Perfect Stranger Series

The Perfect Stranger
The Perfect Cover
The Perfect Lie
The Perfect Life
The Perfect Getaway

The Perfect Stranger Box Set Books 1-5

Wedlocked Trilogy
Dangerous Engagement
Lethal Wedding
Fatal Wedding

Dangerous Engagement Box Set Books 1-3

Lavish Trilogy
Lavish Lies
Lavish Betrayal
Lavish Obsession

Lavish Lies Box Set Books 1-3

All the Lies Series
All the Lies
All the Secrets
All the Doubts

All the Lies Box Set Books 1-3

Not into you Duet

Not into you
Still not into you

Standalone Novels
Dressing Mr. Dalton
Debt
Offer
Unknown

Made in the USA
Las Vegas, NV
22 December 2023

83457422R00177